The Great
Rabbit Revenge Plan

About the author

Burkhard Spinnen was born in Germany in 1956 and lives as a writer in the German city of Münster. He has received many awards for his work, among them the Oldenburg Award for Young Adult Literature and the German Audio Book Award (for *Belgische Riesen,* the German version of *The Great Rabbit Revenge Plan*).

The Great Rabbit Revenge Plan

Burkhard Spinnen

Translated by
Siobhán Parkinson

Little Island

First published 2010
by Little Island
an imprint of New Island
2 Brookside
Dundrum Road
Dublin 14

www.littleisland.ie

First published in Frankfurt am Main, Germany in 2000 by Schöffling & Co.
Verlagsbuchhandlung GmbH.

ISBN 978-1-84840-945-3

Cover illustration © Annie West 2009

Printed in Ireland by Colourbooks

Little Island received financial assistance from
The Arts Council (An Chomhairle Ealaíon), Dublin, Ireland.

J272497
€8.00

The translation of this work was supported by a grant from the Goethe-Institut which is
funded by the German Ministry of Foreign Affairs.

 **GOETHE-INSTITUT**

10 9 8 7 6 5 4 3 2 1

Konrad Makes an Entrance

The door opens.

'By the way,' says Konrad, 'it's totally bright outside.'

It's pretty bright now in the bedroom too, because light is coming in from the landing, and that's how Konrad can see one of the two occupants of the bed swiftly pulling the duvet up over his head. This person says something not very nice, something Konrad would never be allowed to say.

This person is *Dad.* Outside the house, he's called Herr Bantelmann. Inside, of course, Dad. And only very rarely, Wolfgang.

This person was not always Dad. He makes a big deal of this, and he's always making sure Konrad knows all about it. For thirty-one years, Dad was, among other things, a son and a constructor of model aeroplanes. He was the holder of a driving licence. He was the wearer of a beard. And later he was also the *young man* of the other occupant of the big bed.

He's only been Dad for ten years; and although ten years is rather a long time, Dad hasn't quite got used to Dadhood yet. He is least accustomed to Dadhood on Sunday mornings at eight minutes past six. And that's exactly what he says now. What he is saying is perfectly clear, even though he has the duvet over his head. Presumably Dad can see that it is eight minutes past six through a tiny breathing crack that he has left between the mattress and the duvet. It says eight minutes past six in glowing red numbers on the digital alarm clock.

'Konrad,' says Dad's voice from under the duvet, 'what have I forbidden you to do?'

Konrad thinks. Forbidden . . . forbidden? Dad has forbidden pretty well *everything*. How could you possibly know which bit of everything he means at this particular moment?

Luckily, Konrad gets a bit of help. It comes from the person who is lying next to Dad in the bed and who was once his *young lady*. This person is *Mum*. Outside the house, Frau Bantelmann. Inside, of course, Mum; occasionally, Edith.

'It has to do with coming into the bedroom,' she says.

Oh, yes, of course! Konrad gets it immediately. How could he have forgotten? There is a particularly serious rule that has to do with coming into the bedroom on Sunday mornings. You are supposed to, that is to say you should – careful, now, mustn't get this wrong! – on Sunday mornings you should not come in before . . . a particular time. Unfortunately, what this time is escapes Konrad. That is stupid. And so that he won't get it wrong, just to be on the safe side, he says nothing.

Luckily, Mum comes to the rescue again. 'What time is it now?' she says, in a reproachful tone.

Konrad twigs. It looks like he's come in too early, and the time shown on the digital alarm-clock could be a clue as to what time not to come in at. Konrad looks at the clock.

'Nine minutes past six,' he says. At least that much is not wrong.

'Terrific,' says Dad from under the duvet. He makes it sound like a very bad word. 'And what have we forbidden you to do?'

All of a sudden, Konrad remembers. 'I'm not supposed to come in before eight o'clock on Sundays. Except in an emergency – serious illness or fire.' Hey, he'd got it!

'By the way – ' said Konrad.

But Dad roars: 'And what else are you not supposed to do?'

Something comes back to Konrad. You are not, if at all possible, supposed to come into the parental bedroom before eight o'clock on a Sunday morning, and when you do come in, you must absolutely not, never under any circumstances, begin your first sentence with 'by the way'.

Dad has explained it. In fact, he has often explained it. As recently, indeed, as last Sunday. It was round about this time, and Konrad had just come in. The expression 'by the way', Dad had said, is something you use to bring a new subject into a conversation and hook it up to an old subject. He had even demonstrated it, the hooking up, with both hands. Konrad had understood. By the way is a linking expression. It's like this piece of string that you get and you tie two subjects together with it so that they don't fall apart.

'That's right,' Dad had said. And so it follows, as night follows day, that a conversation cannot begin with 'by the way'. For a 'by the way' you need at least two subjects. Two! And on a Sunday morning at however many minutes past six, there is not yet even one subject. In fact there is absolutely no subject whatsoever.

At this point in the explanation, Dad had raised his voice, even though it was so early in the morning. 'No subject!' he'd said. There is no subject, because he, Dad, is not in the middle of a conversation but in the middle of a sleep. And if one of the two future conversationalists is still asleep, then the other conversationalist should bloody well watch out and under no circumstances come barging into the bedroom with a big, thick, fat, ugly 'by the way'.

They'd practised it, last Sunday, the eight o'clock entrance and the beginning of a conversation. Until they'd got it right. Uh-oh. Konrad knows what's coming now. And he is quite correct. 'Get out, and come back in,' says Dad from under the duvet.

'Does he have to?' says Mum. Mum is soft-hearted. She keeps showing it.

'Okay,' says Dad from under the duvet, 'you're the soft-hearted one. Agreed. But who complains most if they can't get a lie-in? You or me?'

Now, this is what Dad always calls a 'rhetorical question'. Rhetorical questions are questions that you don't have to answer, because the answer is already known. And because Mum really does get very cross, in spite of her soft-heartedness, when she can't get a lie-in, she doesn't have to answer now. Konrad considers rhetorical questions very useful. Unfortunately, his parents think up far more of them than he can. And unfortunately, Mum makes a sign to him now, which means 'leave the room and come back in'.

Out on the landing, Konrad paces up and down for a while, so that Mum and Dad have enough time to fall asleep again. They have to be asleep when he comes back in, otherwise it's just not right. On his fourth time up and down, he looks into his younger brother Peter's room and sees that he has kicked his quilt off and is now sleeping on all fours. Konrad takes a closer look. What is he like! His bottom in the air and his head on his forepaws like a sleeping dog. Recently, Mum and Dad were standing by Peter's bed and he'd been sleeping just like this, and Dad had said, 'A natural wonder.' Peter has to hear that. It might amuse him.

'By the way,' Konrad says, 'Dad said you are a natural wonder.' With this, he smacks Peter on his raised bottom.

'Wha-at?'

'A natural wonder. You are a natural wonder.'

'Ugh! What time is it?'

That's another one of those rhetorical questions. Peter is five years old and doesn't know the first thing about the time. He's just repeating what he hears people say. So there's no need to answer. And besides, Konrad has something better to be doing than reading the time for little brothers. He has to make a proper entrance. So, let's go for it!

The first thing he does is to open the bedroom door slowly and carefully, so that Mum and Dad don't get a fright. That's more or less what Dad said. And no sooner has he slipped through the door than he closes it again, so that no unnecessary light falls on Dad. He'd said it was possible that he was a vampire on Sunday mornings, and if vampires get too much light then they crumble into dust and that would be terrible because then Mum would have to brush an enormous pile of dust out of the bed. So now

Konrad is in the room. And it's completely dark. Mum and Dad have recently had new shutters installed and they close so tightly that not even the tiniest streak of light can get in. 'Hermetically sealed,' Dad said and he'd given a funny little laugh.

Konrad, however, is not feeling so very funny in this darkness. He takes a little step and immediately bangs his shin on the bed. It hurts, but at least now he knows where he is. What next? Oh, yes, he must feel his way around the bed until he reaches the crack between the two single mattresses. That's not so hard, and he finds the spot quite quickly. But then it gets more difficult. Because now he has to get into the bed and wriggle his way up the crack on all fours without banging Mum or Dad in a sensitive place with his knee or his elbow or knocking one of Mum's or Dad's teeth out or squashing their noses in with his desperately hard head. The best thing is to keep himself completely flat and to feel his way forward with his hands before wriggling any further. Dad has demonstrated this a few times, but Konrad had unfortunately laughed so hard that tears streamed from his eyes so that he couldn't see a thing.

Anyway, he seems to have reached a head. It's probably Dad's. It's easy to tell Mum's and Dad's heads apart. Mum's face is soft and she has long hair. Dad, on the other hand, has hardly any hair on his head but he is very scratchy in the face. Especially on Sunday mornings, because he doesn't shave on Saturdays.

Konrad gives another feel to be sure. No doubt about it, this is unquestionably Dad. So, he's made it. Now comes the last part of the exercise. It's a bit embarrassing, though.

Konrad likes it very much when someone strokes his hair and whispers something nice into his ear, but to stroke someone else on the head and whisper something into their ear – that he finds rather embarrassing. Good thing it's so dark. Konrad strokes Dad's head and purrs like Aunt Thea's cat. It works. And now to say something nice. Konrad puts his mouth very close to Dad's ear.

Phe-ew! Dad stinks of garlic. Child poison! Mum and Dad were in a restaurant yesterday, and in the restaurants where Mum and Dad go without Konrad and Peter, there's nothing but child poison. The whole menu from beginning to end is child poison with double garlic. Konrad thinks this is terrible. 'By the way,' he says. 'You smell of garlic again.'

'Konrad!' says Mum, and Dad makes a scrunching sound.

Then the door opens and all of a sudden it is bright in the room again.

'By the way,' says Peter. 'I can't help being awake. There!' he points at the bed, where Konrad is by now half sitting on Dad's head. 'Konrad! He woke me up.'

'Great,' says Mum, getting out of bed. 'I'm going to have a shower.'

Dad says something too, but you can't hear what it is, because Konrad has just belted Dad in the face with his knee and Dad is now holding his nose with both hands.

'Will you tell us a story?' asks Peter. He's scrambling into the bed now too, and as he tries to climb over Konrad he gets him in the eye with an elbow. Konrad yells, but only a bit. Then he says, 'Yeah, will you tell us a story?'

And all three, Dad, Konrad and Peter, know that this is indubitably a rhetorical question.

Anabasis the Forest Snake

It's a rhetorical question because Dad cannot possibly answer in any other way except with a heartfelt yes. Because in the first place he always tells Konrad and Peter stories; and secondly he started a new one only yesterday morning. All the same, he doesn't say 'Yes'. Instead, he says, 'You're a pair of tyrants.'

'What are tie-rants?' says Peter.

'Tyrants,' says Dad, 'rule by force.'

'Hmm,' says Konrad.

When Konrad says 'Hmm,' it sounds to strangers as if he means something like, 'Ah, so that's the way it is.' Or 'Oh, great, yes, I see.'

His mum and dad, however, know that he means something quite different. What he means is, 'I haven't the foggiest idea what you are talking about.' Or indeed, 'I don't like that.'

In any case, Dad has to explain the word *tyrants* a bit more precisely.

'In this case,' he says, 'tyrants are persons between five and ten years of age who pay absolutely no attention to their parents' need for sleep.'

Uh-oh. The conversation is starting to get dangerous. Instead of just telling the story, Dad obviously wants to go on talking about what an intolerable impertinence it is to expect a person who is hardly awake yet to tell a story at this hour of the morning. It wouldn't be so bad if it could be a story with an ending. But his dreadful sons expect him to think up – just like that, out of his head, on the spot – a new instalment of a serial story.

Luckily, Konrad is pretty good at changing the subject.

'How big is the snake anyway?' he asks now.

'Seven metres,' says Dad. 'At rest. Nearly nine when it stretches itself out.' He gives a stretch.

Bingo! Now at last they are into the story that started yesterday morning. It is about a forest snake called Anabasis, who is guarding an extraordinary mound of earth deep in a large and impenetrable forest. It's been doing this, night and day, for hundreds of years, and yesterday morning Dad gave an extensive account of which long-extinct animals had come by and asked the snake what it was guarding, to which the snake always replied that it could not say, because it was a great secret.

If Konrad were to be entirely honest, he would have to say that, so far, this snake story doesn't sound all that very promising. It is possible that yesterday morning, Dad had been so tired that nothing else had occurred to him, other than to have some dinosaur or other go past this snake. More or less the way it was in those stupid books Konrad had read before he was able to read. There were all these animals who pestered other animals with questions. A cow who'd lost her little calf, or a crocodile whose baby crocodile had gone missing. The animals who were asked the questions would always say very nicely, 'No thank you, not with me,' or something, until eventually the baby crocodile turned up and all the animals were thrilled in an animal sort of way and the stupid book was finished.

However, Konrad knows that it is not smart to find fault with the first instalment of a new story and to say so out loud. Then Dad would be offended and that in turn would have a bad effect on the quality of the next instalment. And in any case, Konrad plans to make sure that something exciting will happen soon with this forest snake.

So he says, 'Da-ad, what were those people called again who discovered this mound?'

'People?' says Dad.

Possibly he was so tired yesterday morning that he can't remember what he mumbled when he was half asleep. But he doesn't mention that. He just says, 'What people?' instead.

'*You* know, the *people!*' says Konrad.

'Yeah, the *people,*' Peter joins in. And because he always has to move when he talks, he kicks Dad, just a bit, quite unintentionally, in the stomach.

'Oof!' says Dad. 'The people, the people – oh, yes! – it was the people from Forest Expedition Roman Numeral Three Dash Seven, led by the world-famous special scientist Professor Franzkarl Findouter.'

'Aha,' says Konrad. 'Forest Expedition Roman Numeral Three Dash Seven. Right. And the world-famous scientist Franzkarl Findouter.'

This doesn't sound all that very adventurous. But at least it's better than the parade of dinosaurs.

'You have to imagine,' says Dad, 'that by now we've arrived in the twenty-first century. Which is to say, today.'

He pinches Peter on the leg. 'What year is it today?'

'Twenty-two thousand,' says Peter promptly.

'Nearly,' says Dad. 'And just this year a big research centre has decided to send Forest Expedition Roman Numeral Three Dash Seven, led by the aforementioned world famous special scientist Professor Franzkarl Findouter, into the impenetrable forest to figure out the secret of the remarkable mound.'

'But how did they know about this mound?' says Konrad. 'It's in the middle of an impenetrable jungle. You said so yourself.'

Now Dad laughs. Konrad and Peter know this laugh. This is how Dad laughs when he knows something better than anyone else on planet Earth.

How well his sons know him!

'Aerial photography,' he says triumphantly. 'Aerial photographs taken by satellite. With radar!' Using this kind of thing, he explains, you could photograph a lollipop from a height of eighty-three kilometres and you could tell just from looking at the photo whether the lollipop had been licked yet, and if so, by whom. And this is exactly how the people in the research centre discovered this remarkable mound.

'What's a satel-tite?' says Peter.

'Oh, for goodness' sake!' Konrad has known this *forever*. He'd rather know what happens next.

'Stop!' says Dad. It is absolutely correct to ask whenever

there is something that you don't understand. How often has he said this? So he starts to explain, very precisely, what the earth is and what space is and what an orbit of the earth is, and in view of all this, what a satellite must be. But Konrad can't shake off the feeling that Dad is trying to wriggle out of telling the story. At last he gets to the end of the satellite explanation. All this explaining seems to have perked him up a bit, because he plumps up his pillow now and sits up.

'So anyway,' he says, 'Franzkarl Findouter and his expedition arrive at this mysterious mound of earth. These plucky men and women have made enormous efforts to get this far. Only a few hours ago, they sailed the rising waters of the Obernoko in narrow canoes. And the day before, they had almost fallen foul of an attack by warrior ants as long as your finger. But now they have reached their goal. They set up camp, with a little kitchen, and the first thing they do is to make coffee for everyone. They get out the cake and open a tin of custard, they scoff everything, and they have a little nap in the shade, and then – well, then they unpack all their sensitive measuring instruments.'

'Thermometers!' says Peter. 'Like Mum uses to see if you have a fever.'

'That's right,' says Dad. 'They unpack their fever thermometers and their seismographs, their oscilloscopes, their impulse sensors and their spectrum analysis converters. They put them all around the mysterious mound, and they attach them with a cable to a gigantic battery, and then they sit down at their monitors and take a look at what all the gadgets are showing: wonderful sine curves, fabulous parabolic arcs, rhomboidal clusters and strategic agglomerations of data.'

'Hmm,' says Konrad.

Dad ignores the 'Hmm' and goes on with the story. He's really got into the swing of it now. 'And of course,' he says, 'all this cannot happen unbeknownst to Anabasis the forest snake. After all the thousands of years it has spent guarding the secret of the mound, it is now eaten up with anxiety about whether this research team, equipped as it is with all its up-to-the-minute gadgetry, might be able to winkle out the secret.'

Peter moves again, even though he has no idea what he wants to say.

'Lie still!' says Dad. He can't bear being kicked when he is telling a story.

'Go on!' says Konrad.

'Aw,' says Dad, 'the poor old snake.' His voice is shaking slightly, as if he is just about to burst into tears. 'Quaking with terror, it watches, from its hiding place among the branches of a tatyrus tree as the research team researches away quietly around the amazing mound. And all the while, it is trying to think what on earth it can do to chase these wretched intruders away from the mound or, better still, out of the forest altogether.'

Peter suddenly knows what it is that he wants to say. 'The snake!' he says, excitedly. 'The snake, the snake!'

When Peter gets excited, his words start jostling around in his mouth, and because every word wants to be the first one to get out, it often happens that only one or two make it out, and then no more can get out at all. This is the case now, and that's why Dad does what Dad always does when Peter gets clogged up with words. He blows softly into his ear. That tickles, which makes Peter laugh, and then all the words in his mouth get so shaken up that they can finally come out, one after another, from between his lips.

'The snake should buy a tank and shoot the researchers!'

'Really?' No, Dad doesn't like this one little bit. Why do boys always have to suggest so much shooting? That's no solution, to be shooting each other all the time.

Konrad quite agrees. He has a suggestion of his own: 'The snake should bite Franzkarl Findouter in the leg with its poisonous fangs. First, his nervous system will collapse and then he will stop breathing, and after ten minutes he will fall down dead.'

Dad can't understand it. They are supposed to be curious children, interested in finding stuff out! How come they are so quick to take the part of this snake who hates research? Humanity is, after all, entitled to expect that remarkable mounds will be researched.

'How would it be,' says Dad, 'if research wasn't allowed? Without research, there is no knowledge; without research there would be no *Pippi Longstocking* tapes and without research there would be no *Sams* CD. So please, gentlemen, suggest something else!'

'Phew,' says Konrad, and Peter looks as if he is about to burst into tears.

This is not what Dad wanted. 'All right, all right,' he says.

'Maybe you're right. But first you have to find out why the snake is so insistent on keeping the secret of the mound. We have to know this before we can decide what happens next, whether these merry researchers can go on researching away or whether they should disappear from the forest.'

'But what is the secret?' says Konrad.

'But what is the secret?' says Peter.

'The secret,' says Dad. 'The secret – ' He breaks off. 'Did I hear Mum calling us for breakfast?'

'No,' says Konrad. No way had Mum called them for breakfast!

'Well, the secret,' says Dad, 'the secret of the mound is that – '

'Well?'

' – that a gigantic crystal is hidden under it. Ten metres high and five metres across. So,' says Dad, 'now you know!'

'A gigantic crystal!' says Peter.

Maybe it's just a coincidence, but Peter is deeply interested right now in precious stones and crystals and especially in treasure and pirates and stuff like that. And so when an enormous crystal puts in an appearance, he really can't resist some pretty vigorous kicking.

Dad rolls carefully to one side. 'Yes,' he says, 'an enormous crystal, all sparkling with rainbow colours. Pointy on top, and on the bottom more roundy. But of course you can't see that, because more than half of it is stuck in the ground, and there's earth all over the bit that is peeping out as well, so that from the outside, all you can see is this extraordinary mound of earth.

Dad is very proud of his story. When he is proud of his stories he has a certain tone of voice that is very hard to describe.

'Hmm,' says Konrad. 'But why does the snake have to guard the crystal?'

He doesn't get an answer, though. Because now Mum really is calling them for breakfast. At which point, Dad leaps out of bed so quickly that he very nearly kicks Peter in the leg.

The Dransfeld

At breakfast, Konrad sits where he can look out of the window. He sets a lot of store by this. He couldn't bear to miss something going on out on the street.

Actually, the Bantelmanns have only been living in this new house for three weeks, since the beginning of the school holidays. This new house of theirs is surrounded by other new houses, which look very like the Bantelmanns' house, in Hedwig Dransfeld Strasse. And because everything is so new here, Konrad takes an intense interest in even the tiniest details. Three weeks ago, the Bantelmanns were still living on Danziger Strasse, right in the middle of town, on the third floor, the door on the right-hand side. It's a fair bit from Danziger Strasse to Hedwig Dransfeld Strasse. Konrad knows the way very well by now, because while the house was being built, they drove that way hundreds of times. First you drive out of town along Steinbecker Strasse, and the buildings get smaller and smaller as you go. At the last big junction before the canal, there at the new supermarket, you go right, onto the main road. For a while, it looks as if that's it, but then you finally come to Hedwig Dransfeld Strasse. It veers off from the canal road, bends a couple of times for no particular reason, loops around and finally joins up with the main road again.

Until the summer holidays, Konrad was still going to his old school in Frankfurter Strasse, fourth class with Frau Schwenkenberg. But that's all over now, which is a pity because Frankfurter Strasse wasn't very far from Danziger, Frau Schwenkenberg was a nice teacher, and Konrad had friends in his class that he could visit after school. In a few weeks, when the holidays are over, he's going to a new school where he will know nobody. He's seen the school a few times. It's near the new supermarket, and it hasn't been there for very long. Everything is new around here. Even Hedwig Dransfeld Strasse is new. It was built at the same time as the new houses. Before that, the whole area was just a big marsh. Then along came the construction machinery and flattened everything into mud, the building work started, and all the identical houses got built at more or less the same time.

They're what you call duplex houses: every house is for two families and two cars, from number 1a to number 47b. The whole lot together is called the Hedwig Dransfeld Estate, or Dransfeld Estate for short, or shorter still, The Dransfeld.

'Who is this Hedwig Dransfeld?' Konrad asked, two years ago, when they stood for the first time in the middle of the damp field in front of a big hoarding, and Dad read out that soon, Hedwig Dransfeld Strasse, along with forty-seven duplex houses, would be here.

'Was,' Dad said. Frau Dransfeld was, unfortunately, dead. Being dead, Dad explained, is a prerequisite for having a street named after you.

'Hmm,' Konrad said.

The rest of what Dad told him about Frau Dransfeld he couldn't quite remember. Either Frau Dransfeld was a great inventor or she was a politician or she was a witch and was burnt at the stake. It would be best if she had been a witch, of course. Though Konrad wouldn't like to think of her having been burnt at the stake. No one wants to live on a street that was called after someone who was burnt as a witch.

But apart from the name, Dransfeld Strasse is a cool place to live. Starting with the way the houses all look the same. That alone is pretty good fun. While the building was going on, and the houses had no numbers yet at the doors, Konrad regularly went into not their future house, number 17a, but some other house. Peter couldn't work it out at all. Mostly he started to cry as soon as they arrived at the site and began picking their way through the mud. He didn't know his way around, he said. He was only three or four years old.

The houses are all very nice. Upstairs, just over the front door, there's this high, pointy window that lets lots of light onto the landing. Dad often said that the architects deserved special praise for these windows. They made a well-balanced and pleasantly functional yet traditional feature. And then Dad laughed and Mum said, 'Oh, give over.'

What's more, the houses have lovely, brightly painted drainpipes, which wind their way down from the gutters into the front gardens. Here and there, these pipes suddenly break off and they spit their water into a kind of basin, from which it then flows into another pipe. When the rain is really pelting down, this is a wonder to behold, and you forget to be annoyed by the bad weather.

Every house in Dransfeld Strasse has a very small garden in front, and at the back, beyond the patio, a slightly larger one. Before the grass was sown and the beech hedges were planted, these two gardens consisted entirely of wonderful black mud, and for this reason they were out of bounds for Konrad and Peter. Apparently there was a danger that they might bring mud into the house. Which would not be good. Because inside the house, everything is white, or at least very pale. Mud really wouldn't look good in here.

Not only is it all white or pale in the house, but it's completely different from the flat where the Bantelmanns used to live. Even the sockets and the taps and the door handles and the radiators and the skirting boards look different and they feel different too. Konrad and Peter still go around the rooms sometimes, testing out how different everything feels. Mum is not so keen on this.

What's particularly different is that Konrad and Peter now have a room each. The bunk beds that they slept in in Danziger Strasse have been taken apart and made into two beds, and they've got lots of new furniture. Sleeping alone still feels a bit strange, especially for Peter. For this reason, there is a rule that says Konrad is allowed – until the end of the holidays – to stay in Peter's bed until Peter falls asleep after their bedtime story. Or he falls asleep himself. Or they both fall asleep.

When the Bantelmanns were moving in three weeks ago, their removal van was hardly able to find a parking spot. The Dransfeld looked like a reunion of removal-van owners. All the Dransfelders were trying to move into their new houses at the same time. This made everyone cross, because they kept treading on each other's toes and it was even rumoured that some furniture was moved into the wrong house. What with one thing and another, the whole business of moving in took much longer than expected. Packing cases were still being sorted out late into the night, and then the van drivers had to make a big hoo-ha about getting their vans out of The Dransfeld without bashing into each other.

From the very first day they moved in, Konrad began a careful investigation of The Dransfeld. He wrote up his research findings in a homework notebook where only one page had been written on. He tore that one out, and on the next page he wrote *Dransfeld Investigation*. And since then, he has been taking notes in the notebook. Konrad's first observation was that not only do the houses all look the same, but the new inhabitants also resemble each other. For example, they all have a Volkswagen Passat or at least a car that looks a bit like that. At any rate, it has to be a long one, with a hatchback. And on the back window there has to be a 'Baby on Board' sticker. Either a new one, or one that's half worn away, or one that's all pale and washed-out looking from the car wash.

Apart from that, there has to be a father and a mother in each duplex half and they always have two children. Which is to say, some have only one child and a few have three, but they mostly have two, and if the ones who have three gave one of theirs to the ones who have only one, then they would all have two. Konrad worked that out in his notebook, using the law of averages, and it came out almost exactly. Although of course a few of the mothers could have a new baby, and that would mess up his calculations.

Not that that would be a problem. The great thing is that suddenly he and Peter have got lots of kids to play with. Do the maths: forty-seven duplexes multiplied by two families multiplied by two children makes a hundred and eighty-eight children, all within easy walking distance!

When they'd lived in the big apartment house in Danziger Strasse, there was no one to play with. Philip lived three whole buildings away, and it was so far to Justus's house that Konrad hadn't been allowed to go there on his own until he was in third class. Before that, Mum or Dad had to take him round and pick him up, and they would mutter about a child-friendly environment.

Konrad knows what that is now. Soon he'll know so many children in The Dransfeld that he could, theoretically speaking, play with a different child every second day for a whole year. More or less. Of course, Konrad hasn't managed to meet all the other children in the space of three weeks, but soon he will have.

It's very easy to meet all the kids in The Dransfeld, one by one. The front doors are left open everywhere, because people are still bringing stuff in or because they are working in their little front gardens. And the easiest way to get to know other children quickly is to wander straight from number 17a in through one of the open doors. Konrad goes through the hall and up the stairs. Upstairs there are two doors beside each other. In the A houses, they are on the right, and in the B houses on the left. These are the children's rooms. In every house it's the same, and on most of the doors the children's names are already stuck on in brightly painted wooden letters. This way, Konrad can tell if a boy or a girl lives on the other side of the door, and what their name is. If it's a girl – sometimes it's two – too bad, because of course you can't play with girls. Then Konrad goes downstairs again, softly, softly, and gets out of there without being seen, if possible.

If it's a boy, though, then all he has to do is knock on the door and if someone calls out, 'Come in!' then he goes in and says, 'Hello, Sebastian, I'm Konrad from number 17a,' or 'Hello, Christoph,' 'Hello Fabian,' 'Hello Viktor,' or whatever. And then it all goes on from there.

Since last week, Konrad has been taking Peter along on these visits. Sometimes the boys weren't the right age. Once, Konrad knocked on the door of a Michael, and he called out good and loud, 'Come in!' but then there was this rather young boy sitting on a blue carpet playing with these biggish wooden blocks. That was embarrassing. And as if that wasn't bad enough, this mother has to appear in the doorway and say how nice it is that someone has dropped in to play with Michael, and Konrad had to sit on the blue carpet for two solid hours, playing with the biggish blocks. To make sure that doesn't happen again, he brings Peter along, and if there turns out to be a little chap on the other side of the door, then all Konrad has to say is, 'Hello, Michael, this is my brother Peter. Would you like to play together?' If they want to, and they always do, then Konrad can leave his little brother there and scoot off to the next open door and the next child of the right age.

It's not a bit dangerous. You wouldn't usually take your little brother by the hand and leave him with strangers. Anything but! But here in The Dransfeld the rules are different. Dad said so. Here you are completely secure, and everyone is there for everyone else. Dad said this on their second evening in The Dransfeld, while they were having dinner and fifty people rang on the door, one by one, to let him know that his Passat headlamps were on. 'That's what they're like,' Dad said, 'the people who have moved into The Dransfeld, always watching out for their neighbours!' You could leave your little brother with these people without giving it a second thought. Either someone would pick him up later, or the people themselves would drop him home.

Mum and Dad are completely in agreement with this procedure, because when the neighbours bring Peter home, they usually stay for a while. In fact, Mum always asks them in. They get something to eat and to drink. They don't want anything, they always say, but they do eat and drink anyway, and they talk too. Mostly they talk about what works especially well in their house or what doesn't work. For example, the underfloor heating is a dream, but the windows that you are supposed to be able to open at the top are a catastrophe. Or they tell about the problems they have with the people who live in the other half of their duplex. They say it is impossible to get them to agree where the compost bin should go and where to put the ordinary rubbish bin. Or they just explain who they are and what they do and especially what they like in life and what they don't like.

'Take Peter anywhere you like,' Dad said. According to

him, it's very refreshing to meet so many people with so many different problems. You get a whole new view of the world. He had more to say, but Mum somehow managed to make him shut up.

Since last week, Konrad has been bringing not only his younger brother on these Dransfeld expeditions, but also an elaborate list of the children he has already met. That became necessary when Konrad twice went into houses where he had already been. Both times, houses with girls! This new list is of course written in The Dransfeld notebook. It takes up several pages and has lots of columns. In the leftmost column there's just a number. That's the house number. Konrad has carefully written in all the numbers from 1a to 47b. In the next column is a name: Christoph or Sebastian or Viktor or Julian; these are the children who live in the houses. Of course, only the names of those who would make good playmates are written in, in other words, boys of the right age. Where there are only girls, Konrad puts a big red stroke. The most important column, however, by a long shot, is the third. Because here it says what the kids' favourite things to do are, and what they hate doing. After the name Christoph, for example, it says, 'doesn't like Lego'. And after Sebastian, 'has *Crazy Bugs 2*', and after Viktor, 'can do good stuff'.

Every time Konrad makes a new visit, he makes a new entry in his list. It'll soon be finished. And then it will be very useful. If, for example, he doesn't feel like playing Lego, then he can see that it would be a good idea to go round to Christoph's, because he doesn't like Lego. And if he is bursting to play *Crazy Bugs 2*, then it's off to

Sebastian's, because he is constantly at the computer. And so on and so forth.

The fourth column is also pretty important. The one on the far right. Here it says who has a little brother who likes playing with Peter. That's someplace you can go, take Peter along, and at the same time, you haven't got him under your feet all day. And then when you get home in the evening, you've been looking after your little brother all afternoon, for which you get the highest possible praise.

Yesterday, Mum and Dad saw the list for the first time, when Konrad was making an entry at breakfast. They both read the list, and they reacted completely differently. Which is pretty unusual. Dad covered his face with his hands and left the room, saying his son had fallen victim to consumerism to such an extent that he was turning his neighbours into a mail-order catalogue. Konrad didn't quite follow this. Mum, on the other hand, said there was no need to get so het up, and anyway it had been a great idea to move into The Dransfeld. All the same, Konrad didn't bring the list with him to breakfast this morning, in order to avoid as much conflict as possible, especially on Sunday morning when the family has to decide what to do today.

'Zoo!' says Peter.

A good suggestion. And because the Bantelmanns have a yearly ticket for the zoo, and because the yearly ticket is only worth it if you go to the zoo fairly often, they all agree.

Out of sheer delight, Peter knocks over his drinking chocolate.

Rivals on the Obernoko

Every evening, when they go to bed, Konrad and Peter are asked what the best thing was about the day, and what the silliest thing was. Dad and Mum started doing this because it's a great help in bringing up their wonderful sons.

Well, then?

'The zoo,' says Peter. He's lying in bed on the wall side and pushing in the face of his cuddly mouse. The mouse is called Lackilug and it's fairly old and has a little bell round its neck.

'Can you be a bit more specific?' says Dad, who is lying in the middle of Peter's bed.

'The animals,' says Konrad, who is lying on the falling-out side of Peter's bed. He has his toy mouse tucked, in the approved manner, under his arm. For reasons that are lost in the mists of time, his mouse is called Mattchoo, with a double-t and a double-o. It is considerably older than Lackilug, and looks it.

'Not specific enough!'

That's always the way. When the children want something, then talk comes bubbling up out of them, but when their parents want them to answer a question, then their little mouths are all zipped up. That's what Dad says right now.

'The elephants,' says Peter.

Which is exactly what you would expect him to say. Peter had been unbelievably brave today at feeding the elephants. First he took the biggest piece of stale bread that you could buy from the elephant keeper and he didn't let go of it until the elephant had got hold of it good and proper with its trunk. He was masterly. The other children screamed and let go of the bread as soon as the big hairy trunk tried to get hold of it, and it kept falling into the muck. But Peter held on till the elephant had got half his trunk round the piece of bread. And not until the elephant started to tug on Peter himself and his parents were beginning to scream a bit did Peter let go of the bread so that the elephant could whisk it elegantly into its mouth.

Encore! Bravo!

'And the silliest thing?' says Mum. She's sitting at the foot of the bed. There's a bit of room left there.

Inevitably, the knocking over of the drinking chocolate at breakfast gets mentioned. Because that was undoubtedly the silliest thing this Sunday. The Bantelmanns have been discussing the knocking over of drinking chocolate for years. That is to say, for years, the Bantelmann parents have been trying to convince Peter that the chocolate can't help it if it is knocked over. Peter, however, always has some new reason why it is not his fault but the fault of the stupid chocolate itself that it has fallen over. So what's his excuse going to be today?

'It was standing all wrong!' says Peter.

Not very imaginative.

'It wasn't standing wrong. It was put down wrong.'

'But it was wobbling!'

Not much better.

'It wasn't wobbling. It was wobbled.'

Konrad has to laugh. It sounds so weird: it was wobbled. You can't say that!

'That was a joke,' says Dad. But he's looking grim enough.

'I'm allergic to jokes,' says Peter. He pushes Lackilug's face in again.

'True,' says Mum, 'but the tablecloth is allergic to chocolate. It breaks out in terrible spots from chocolate.'

'And sunburn!' Konrad laughs even louder.

If one more joke is made about the tipping over of the chocolate, Peter is sure to cry. You can tell by looking at him, Mum says. She can read Peter's and Konrad's faces like a book. Especially when they are telling lies.

Konrad can't do this. One time he stood in front of the mirror and said loudly, 'We have a red Golf.' That was a lie, because they have a blue Passat. In any case, there was nothing whatever to be seen in his face. He told Mum this.

'I mean it metaphorically,' said Mum. 'Sometimes people say something that doesn't mean what it seems to mean, but means something else, in a transferred kind of way.'

'Hmm,' Konrad said.

'Okay,' says Dad. 'Let's just leave it at that for now.'

Mum says good night.

'So, where were we?' says Dad.

At the secret of the crystal, of course. And the question of why the forest snake had to guard it.

'Well,' says Dad. 'It's hard to say. To be honest – the snake doesn't know why it is supposed to guard the crystal.'

'Hmm,' says Konrad.

There's no doubt about it, this forest snake story just hasn't got any pizzazz.

'Or to put it more accurately,' says Dad, 'the forest snake does know that it is supposed to guard the crystal, and that this is its most important task, but what it doesn't know is why it has to guard the crystal. Basically, it's a bit like Peter and knocking the chocolate over. We do know that he always knocks it over, but we don't know why he does it. Ha ha, ha ha!'

No one laughs except Dad.

'Right,' he says. 'So, anyway, the forest snake is a bit nervous, because there is something that it has to do. At this stage, the members of the expedition have got all excited because their sensitive instruments – '

'Thermometers!' Peter interrupts.

' – right, because their sensitive thermometers are giving the most astonishing readings. Obviously, there is some sort of compacted and impenetrable lump of something under the extraordinary mound. A rare substance. Maybe a substance that has not yet been discovered. In a word, a sensational find. The scientists are totally out of their trees. "The Nobble Prize!" they keep shouting, "The Nobble Prize is ours!"'

'What's the Nobble Prize?' asks Peter from behind Lackilug the mouse.

'You get the Nobble Prize for important discoveries and inventions,' says Dad. 'It was founded by Ernst August

Nobble, the inventor of the game of Ludo, and it is awarded once a year.'

'Huh?' says Konrad. 'Huh' is a more intense form of 'Hmm'.

'Yes,' says Dad. 'Of course you know Ludo, widely agreed to be the most boring and depressing board game in the whole world. The game that makes Peter and Konrad Bantelmann whinge way more than all other boardgames put together. Ernst August Nobble invented this game. And when he heard later how children all over the world cry when they are knocked out of the game just as they are about to reach Home, and how the mothers and fathers get so bored that it drives them mad, then Ernst August Nobble looked into his soul and he said he wanted to make amends and that he wanted to establish a terrific prize that would really do something great for humanity.'

'Hmm,' says Konrad.

'Exactly,' says Dad. 'And of course, every scientist wants to get this Nobble Prize. Including Professor Franzkarl Findouter. But!' Dad raises a finger. 'Here it comes! There is another scientist who wants it even more than Franzkarl Findouter. And that is none other than the mysterious Dr B. A. Deceiver.'

'Be a?' says Peter.

'Yes. B for Bigomil. His full name is Bigomil Alexander Deceiver. For days, he has secretly been following the troop of researchers. This B. A. Deceiver is nothing like as gifted an expert as Franzkarl Findouter. In fact, he's a bit of a lazybones, and ambitious to boot, as ambitious as it gets.

Even as a boy at school, he copied everything. He gave his lunch to the people he copied from. He wouldn't have eaten it anyway because it was always cheese sandwiches and he couldn't for the life of him abide cheese sandwiches.'

'I can't stand cheese either,' says Konrad.

'That was only in passing,' says Dad.

'What's "in passing"?'

'It has to do with football,' says Peter through the mouse.

'Right,' says Dad, 'That's enough of that. Back to Dr B. A. Deceiver. He's watching now from a hiding place and he sees that the research team is thrilled to bits about their instrument readings. And he decides right away to nab this sensational find all for himself and to make it so that he gets the Nobble Prize and not this fussy old Franzkarl Findouter.'

'He's mean,' says Peter. But it's very hard to know what he is saying, because he has his mouth half full of Lackilug.

Dad pulls the mouse out, which makes its little bell ring, and he gives Peter a lecture about what he thinks of five-year-old boys who first of all breathe through their soft toys and then try to eat them. An uninteresting lecture. But just to be on the safe side, Konrad stuffs his soft toy, the mouse with the annoying name of Mattchoo, a little bit further down under the duvet. Dad takes an even poorer view of this mouse, a: because it is old and therefore a bit shabby, and b: because it is called what it is called. But since he can't explain to his son why this is such an impossible name for a cuddly toy, Konrad goes right on refusing to give his toy another name.

'Is it a quarter past yet?' says Dad.

At a quarter past eight, bedtime stories are over. And so that everyone can see when the time has come, there's a clock by the door, with a grinning little man on it whose arms form the hands that point to the numbers. An embarrassing clock.

But he's trying to catch Konrad out. Dad can see the clock quite as easily as the boys can. He just wants to see if Konrad can read the time.

Of course Konrad can read the time. For sure! At his age! But lately, there's this rumour in the Bantelmann family that he can't. It has something to do with coming in so early on Sunday mornings. But it's only that he is a bit absent-minded, because his head is so full of Dransfeld thoughts. Even so, it's a bit difficult to read the time just now, because everything is difficult when somebody is standing over you – or in this case, is lying beside you – to check whether or not you can do whatever it is. Especially such a jumpy, watchful checker. Nobody can do anything right when there's a checker there.

'Eleven minutes past eight,' says Konrad now.

'Well, well,' says Dad.

So he must have got it roughly right.

'Back to Dr B. A. Deceiver. While the research squad are asleep in their tents dreaming of the Nobble Prize, he creeps, under cover of darkness, out of his hiding place to the curious mound of earth. He's brought a little shovel with him, an ice pick and a little bucket. His outrageous plan is to dig his way through to the mysterious substance and then to hack out a piece of it with his ice pick and to carry it off in his bucket. The following morning, he's planning to cross the Obernoko in utter secrecy, go home on the next jungle bus and pocket the Nobble Prize.'

'Pocket?' says Konrad.

'Yes. Pocket, nab, snatch. Cream it all off for himself.'

'Oh, right.'

'But!' says Dad, with a quiver in his voice. 'But the wily Deceiver hasn't reckoned with Anabasis the forest snake. When it sees the sneaky scientist creeping towards the earth mound, it slithers as fast as it can after him. And when the baddie is just about to start digging at the top of the mound, it wraps itself around his feet seven times. Deceiver gets such a shock that he nearly dies on the spot. What is that on his feet? In the dark, he can't make it out. Heeyy!'

Dad grabs Peter by the feet. Peter screeches.

'Quiet,' says Dad. 'Deceiver can't screech, because that would wake up the others. Instead, he tries to run away, but try running away with a seven-metre-long forest snake wound round your legs seven times! Ha ha! He can't get away, not even a metre. He comes crashing down the mound like a level-crossing barrier and drops his shovel, his bucket and his ice pick. When he arrives at the bottom, Anabasis the forest snake unwinds itself from his legs and disappears soundlessly into the jungle so that Deceiver thinks that it must have been a ghost or a ghoul or some kind of a spooky thing that has felled him so painfully. In any case, he doesn't say a word and retreats, shaking, to his hiding place, crawls into his sleeping bag and pulls the zip up so far that he almost gets his nose stuck in it.

'Hoi,' says Konrad. That's another more intense form of 'Hmm'. He'd never have believed that something as exciting as that could happen in this forest snake story.

'And that's all for tonight,' says Dad. 'It's exactly a quarter past eight.'

He stands up, which is not so very simple. You could easily stand on a child.

'Besides,' he says, 'you have to stop when it's at the most exciting point.' The boys don't agree. Nor does Lackilug or Mattchoo. When the light goes out and Konrad, as usual, stays on for a while in Peter's bed, the two mice discuss the story so far. They seem to be very edgy, and possibly they are of different minds. But an outsider can't be sure about that, because Mattchoo and Lackilug converse in a totally incomprehensible language, which sounds a bit as if someone had turned the speed way up on a cassette player. It's a cross between squeaking and squealing. Konrad calls it muggering. But he doesn't tell anyone this, not even Peter.

Fridz with a D

After Sunday comes Monday. Too bad. There it is and there is nothing to be done about it. Konrad has known this for ages. Peter knows it too, but on some Sunday evenings, he still asks what day tomorrow is. Maybe he thinks that it changes every five years, and the next change might be that Saturday is going to start coming after Sunday.

This Monday is not so bad, though. Because it's still the holidays, so Konrad has the whole day to fill in his list of children. Everyone in The Dransfeld is on holidays. Elsewhere people go jetting off all over the world in every direction on the first day of the holidays, leaping around like cows that have been bitten by ants, to take their so-called vacations in places where there is no one for their children to play with. The Dransfelders, however, will not be going anywhere for years because they have to pay off the mortgages on their lovely houses. That's what Dad says at breakfast with a sigh.

'Mortgages?' asks Konrad.

'Mortgage' is a word that means you don't have *more,* you have less, because you have to keep paying for your house. You don't have enough to pay for it all at once, so you pay for it in little bits for a very long time until it's all paid for, and while you are paying it off, you have less money for other things. 'Just like us,' Dad had said, and then he and Mum had looked sadly at each other.

There is something else that's good about this Monday. Konrad doesn't have to take Peter with him, because Peter has to go to the dentist with Mum, straight after breakfast. That's rough on Peter, but he is in good form. He's never been to the dentist before and hasn't got a clue what awaits him. Mum and Dad have strictly forbidden Konrad to talk to Peter about teeth and dentists. There'll be plenty of time for that later.

When Mum and Peter have left, Konrad takes a quick look at his list. Then he sticks The Dransfeld notebook in the right-hand pocket of his trousers and off he goes.

On Saturday, he'd got as far as number 27b. That means it's number 28a today, which is at the end of Dransfeld Crescent. Number 27b had been something of a disappointment. He'd got in without being noticed, but then there were two girls' names on the children's doors, two very similar names: Lena and Lisa. Konrad is clued in to this sort of thing: they have to be twins! He was out of there like greased lightning. Luckily, no one saw him. Two girls! And twins to boot! Unthinkable! A girl is bad enough, and two girls are more than twice as bad as one, but twin girls – that takes the biscuit for terribleness!

He doesn't quite know why girls are so awful, and why you can't play with them. But all the boys at school are always saying so, and if everyone says so, then it has to be true. In fact, Konrad did once play with a girl. It was in second class, and it probably happened by mistake. He'd probably forgotten for a moment that boys just don't play with girls. Konrad remembers it well. It was during break one day, when it was raining. This girl Charlotte came up to him. She sat two desks away from him and she usually wore her hair in plaits.

'Will you play dots-and-boxes?' she asked. And he, Konrad-head-in-the-clouds, said, thick as anything, 'Yes', and he played away at dots-and-boxes with her, not thinking anything of it, until Philip came by, tapped him on the arm and said, 'Ha ha!'. Then, of course, he came to and realised he was playing with a girl, and that was the end of that.

Konrad is outside number 28a now. But hey! What's wrong here? Number 28a looks just like the other houses in The Dransfeld. But right next door, number 28b – that's a house that's in a class of its own! Konrad can see that at a glance. For example, there is no tiny little beech hedge growing along by the path to the front door. In fact, there is nothing at all growing in the front garden, and the lovely black earth is just lying there, all driven over by the construction vehicles. Konrad takes a closer look. The kitchen window has no flower-patterned net curtains. There is no artistic nameplate at the door, just a lump of sticky tape with the name 'Frenke' written on it with a marker. And instead of a mat saying 'Welcome' there's a dirtyish rag on the doorstep. Good heavens!

Konrad takes a few steps towards the garage. Unbelievable! There is no Passat in the drive, no hatchback of any description, only a weird, clapped-out, boxy contraption that hardly looks like a car at all. A bit like an upturned old-fashioned pram. And in the garage? Konrad goes past the clapped-out car. In the garage there is no rack where you hang your gardening tools nice and tidily. And no wheel around which you coil your garden hose. But there's something else! Right at the back of the garage is a cage made of wood and wire meshing. It has three levels and little doors and it is mounted on six legs. A cage in a Dransfeld garage! Konrad is so surprised that he goes right up to it, without thinking, to take a closer look.

At first, he thinks the hutch is empty. It's quite murky in the garage. But then he sees THE BEAST! It's probably some kind of rabbit, but Konrad has never seen a rabbit like this. It's so big! Unbelievably big. It's sitting in the middle storey of the cage, right at the back, in a corner, and it is not moving. It's just doing something with its nose. It probably can't move, it's so huge. It can't even prick up its enormous ears, because they would bang against the ceiling of the cage.

Konrad's eyes are gradually getting used to the dark. Ah, so that's what the creature is doing with its nose. It's eating a carrot. Beside it there are more carrots, more than Konrad could eat in a lifetime. But the way this giant rabbit is putting it away, there's probably just about enough to keep it going for half an hour at most.

'Hey, you,' says a voice suddenly, and a hand touches Konrad's head from behind. Just as he turns around, Konrad notices that he is blushing. Hopefully there is not going to be trouble. It's not exactly polite to go stomping into other people's garages. But when Konrad has fully turned around, he realises that there isn't going to be trouble. The woman standing in front of him looks completely different from the other Dransfeld mothers – and Konrad is sure she isn't going to be cross with him. The woman is very slim and she has very long dark red hair. Her face is pale and she's wearing very dark lipstick. Her eyes are also heavily made-up. She's wearing purple trousers and a T-shirt with so many crazy flowers on it that it nearly makes Konrad laugh. All the same, the woman looks kind of sad.

'Have you come to visit us?' she asks.

Konrad nods.

'You're Konrad, aren't you?'

How on earth does she know that? Konrad shrinks back a bit. Are his Dransfeld investigations common knowledge? Just to be on the safe side, he puts his right hand over his pocket so that there is no way his notebook can fall out.

'I haven't got much time at the moment,' says the woman. But he can go on in, she says. Fritz is upstairs.

Konrad can't think of anything to say to that. So he just makes a little gesture with his hand and goes on into number 28b.

He can hardly believe his eyes! Inside, it's just as different as outside. For a start, the packing cases are still lying around. Imagine: packing cases! After three whole weeks. Mum and Dad Bantelmann are still talking about how they had completely unpacked all their crates within thirty-six hours of moving in. And folded them up.

That's not the only thing. The furniture in the hall and in the large living room of number 28b looks as if it hasn't been put in its proper place yet. It's standing around in groups, probably discussing how it should spread itself around. Moreover, there is not the smallest picture hanging on the wall, and there isn't a single plant on any of the windowsills. Not to mention a china goose lit from within, or a bunch of tulips made of painted wood.

Otherwise, Konrad feels quite at home. Up the stairs he goes to the two doors. At least this much is the same as in all the other houses. But now there's another problem. There are, of course, no names on the doors. Konrad thinks. The mother mentioned a Fritz. And if this Fritz were either much too young or much too old for him, then she'd surely have said so. So Konrad knocks first on the door to the left.

'Come in!'

A perfectly ordinary 'Come in!' Or maybe not? Konrad turns the handle and goes in, and – there on the floor is a girl holding a doll in her hands. Oh no! How bad can it get! But it's too late to get out of this one. He just has to get on with it.

'Sorry,' says Konrad. 'I'm looking for Fritz.'

'I'm Fridz,' says the girl. 'My real name is Friederike. Friederike Caroline Luise Frenke. But Friederike is for later, when I'm old and dead.'

'Hmm,' says Konrad.

The girl stands up. 'Until recently, I was called Fritzi, a very common short form of Friederike. But I can't have that any longer! You know, that silly i at the end – other girls can keep it. Now I'm called Fridz. But with a d, to make the difference. D'you see?'

'Ah,' says Konrad. He sees nothing.

Fridz reaches out and shakes his hand. 'And who are you?'

'Konrad,' says Konrad. 'Number 17a.'

'Number 17a?' says Fridz. 'That's not much of a name either.'

'What?' says Konrad.

'Joke.'

'Oh, right.' Konrad stands and stares. This Fridz looks quite like her mother. She's very pale, she has the same long, red hair and her T-shirt is covered in crazy flowers. Though she also has freckles and she doesn't look sad. Cheeky, more like.

'And you?' she says. 'What do they call you? Konni, maybe?'

Oh, for goodness' sake! What on earth has he let himself in for?

'No,' says Konrad. Come off it! It's been years since he got his mother to stop calling him Konni. He can't let it all start up again now!

'Radi maybe?'

Hell's bells! It's about time the subject was changed. Otherwise, things are going to get more and more embarrassing. But how is he going to make this happen? Ah, yes!

'Is that your rabbit?' asks Konrad. 'The one down in the garage?'

'Hmm,' says Fridz.

Does 'Hmm' mean the same thing when she says it as when he does? Hard to know.

'It's pretty fat,' says Konrad.

'D'you want to see him?'

Well, it's worked. Because now Konrad can say, 'Sure, I want to see him,' and then they can go downstairs, and then he'll be outside again. The rest will be easy, and in five minutes at the most he'll be able to get out of here. Lucky!

'Sure, I want to see him,' says Konrad.

Fridz throws the doll on the bed. 'Right then, let's go.'

Downstairs, they meet her mother again. She's sitting at a table that almost totally blocks the doorway from the hall into the kitchen. How stupid is that! thinks Konrad. At home, they're always saying how handy this wide doorway is. And here they block it up with a table!

The mother has a piece of paper in front of her, a letter, which she is reading. She's holding her head up with her hands and her long red hair falls to the left and right of the letter onto the table.

'We're just going out,' says Fridz.

'Go ahead,' says her mother. 'But don't forget, we have to leave in ten minutes.'

In the garage Fridz opens one of the doors of the rabbit hutch. The great, big, fat rabbit drops his carrot and takes a leap that shakes the whole cage. But Fridz is faster, and she's got him by the back. Now the animal is quiet again and lets itself be taken out of the cage.

'There,' says Fridz. 'Hold him for a minute!'

And before Konrad has time to think, never mind say anything, he is holding the gigantic rabbit. He needs to use two hands and press the thing against his chest. It's heavier than a schoolbag.

'No need to be afraid,' says Fridz. 'He won't do anything.'

That's obviously a lie. His head, with those enormous ears, is lying just beside Konrad's head and the creature immediately starts doing something to Konrad's ear with its nose. Something that sends the owner of the ear totally crazy. Because firstly, he is suddenly overcome by the fear that his ear is going to be gobbled up like one of the carrots, and secondly, it tickles so much that he wants to roar laughing. And thirdly, he knows that there are two things he absolutely must not do: roar and drop this monster rabbit. Which means that he has to keep still – even if it costs him his ear.

'Here, give him back to me,' says Fridz at last, grabbing the rabbit and bundling it back into the cage.

'It's a Flemish Giant,' she says. 'There used to be five. This lad here is the last of them.'

'Oh, right,' says Konrad, wishing he could wash his ear. But he doesn't say this out loud. He's glad that at least it is still attached to his head. 'Is he yours?' he says instead.

'Yes and no.'

And then Konrad puts his foot in it. Probably because he's so happy that he has managed to hang onto his ear. He doesn't say, 'Well, goodbye then!' or something like that so he can clear off out of there. Instead he asks, 'What's that supposed to mean, "yes and no"?'

'Yes and no means yes and no,' says Fridz. 'No, because the rabbits actually belong to my father. And yes, because my father has left us, and since he can't bring himself to part from this one, I have to look after it.'

So that was it! Her father had gone off. Konrad is really up to his neck in it now. And now he can't possibly just say, 'Well, goodbye then!' and scoot off. That would be rude. Worse, that would be cold and horrible.

'Hmm,' he says. 'Your father has left you?'

'Yeah,' says Fridz. She takes a not quite fresh-looking lettuce out of a box, tears a few leaves off it and throws them into the hutch.

'Just like that?' says Konrad.

'Just like that? Just like that! Are you thick or what?'

'I'm only asking.'

'Of course not just like that.' Fridz sticks her finger through the meshing to make the rabbit come close enough for her to run her fingers through its fur.

'So what's the story, then?' says Konrad.

'Bah,' says Fridz. 'Mum and Dad don't love each other any more. Shortly before we moved in here, they decided to separate. That's all.'

'Oh,' says Konrad. 'So that's why your packing cases haven't all been unpacked yet?'

'If that was all, it wouldn't be so bad,' says Fridz. 'Everything is upside down. Mum sits for half the day at the kitchen table crying. She can't manage anything. At least it's the holidays.'

Konrad finally spots an opportunity to steer the conversation in a different direction.

'Will you be going to school here too?' he says.

'Sure. Where else would I go?'

'What class are you going into?'

'Fifth.'

'Hey!' says Konrad. 'Me too! We can walk together in the mornings.'

Oh no! How did he let this sentence out of his mouth? Walking to school with a girl! That'll make a fine impression in his new class. But on the other hand, Konrad wants to say something nice to this girl. He's not quite sure why.

'Yeah, sure we can.'

She says nothing more for a while, and then she says, 'By the way, I can't do anything today. I have to go with Mum to see her solicitor. But I'll have time tomorrow. Will you come over tomorrow?'

For the second time today, Konrad is aware that he is blushing. Oh, you great big idiot! What is this going to lead to? To carrying a fat rabbit around, that's what. Or even to playing with dolls! What can he say? There is one possible solution. 'Have you got a computer?' he asks carefully. It must sound as if there is no question of his hanging around with people who haven't got a computer.

'Sure,' says Fridz. 'I have my dad's old one. And I have *Crazy Bugs 3*.'

'What?!' cries Konrad. 'Is *Crazy Bugs 3* out already?'

'Sure. Haven't you seen it? On level four, there are much bigger nets. Hey, listen, let's meet up tomorrow after lunch, say about two?'

Konrad nods.

'Well, bye then,' says Fridz. She gives a little wave and disappears into the house.

Five minutes later, Konrad Bantelmann is walking very

slowly all the way along Hedwig Dransfeld Strasse with his list of children in his pocket. He is making for 17a. He has no interest any more in checking out number 28a or number 29a or any other number. All he can do is repeat to himself over and over again, 'I have a date with a girl. I have a date with a girl.'

When he arrives at number 17a, the blue Passat is just pulling up. Out of it come a pretty rattled-looking Mum and a pretty tearful-looking Peter. Konrad just stands on the pavement and says, quite loudly by way of greeting, 'By the way, I have a date with a girl tomorrow.'

'Don't worry,' says Mum. 'Everyone has to go through it at some stage.'

'She's called Friederike, but she calls herself Fridz. Fridz with a d.'

'You'd want to watch out,' says Mum. 'That sounds pretty frisky for starters.'

Then she takes the tearful Peter in her arms and carries him into the house. Konrad remains standing on the pavement. He stares at the little beech hedge in the front garden of number 17a and at the flowery net curtains in the kitchen window and at the nameplate on which the names of the Bantelmanns are written in loopy writing. Tomorrow, 28b. What has he let himself in for?

The Jelly Crystal

On the evening of this thought-provoking Monday, the mood in the Bantelmanns' house is a bit tense. Peter has been crying all afternoon, more or less. No, he says, it doesn't hurt any more. But he only has to think of the dentist, and the tears just come, he can't help it. But Mum swears it can't hurt now, nor can it have hurt before, because the dentist did nothing except look in Peter's mouth and say that everything is fine. But Peter won't hear of it. He has somehow got hold of the idea that going to the dentist is a dreadful thing, even if he doesn't go near your teeth. Konrad views his younger brother with respect. Smart lad.

Dad is not in a great mood either. He's been to the bank, and they recalculated how long it is going to take to pay off the mortgage on the new house. Completely. Including interest. Interest is a stupid word, anyway. What is so interesting about wringing money out of people? In any event, the calculations were not a lot of fun and Dad said a few things that Mum definitely did not want to hear.

Konrad hasn't exactly had the most amusing afternoon of his life either. Quite the opposite. In the first place, he spent a lot of time repeating the sentence 'I have a date with a girl,' and every time, it sounded worse than before. And then he wanted to work on his list, and that wasn't so very thrilling either, because after '28b' and 'Fridz (with a d)', he had to put in the third column 'has *Crazy Bugs 3*' and 'has a horrible rabbit', two things that don't really go together. The worst thing, though, was that he also had to write in the third column 'is a girl'. There was hardly any room for it, and afterwards, he felt as if the whole list had been ruined.

At least he had the rest of the story of the forest snake to look forward to.

'Where were we?' says Dad, lying down between the two boys.

'At Dr B. A. Deceiver,' says Konrad.

'That's right,' says Dad. 'We finished yesterday with the account of how Anabasis, the forest snake, successfully foiled Deceiver's attempt to gain possession of the crystal and to steal the scientific work of the great Professor Franzkarl Findouter.'

'Hmm,' says Konrad. 'By the way, is Findouter married?'

'I beg your pardon?' says Dad.

'Is Findouter married?' Konrad repeated. He wriggles up a bit higher as he speaks and accidentally kicks Dad someplace.

'Since you ask,' says Dad, 'I'd say ... well, I'd say Franzkarl Findouter has been married for the past twelve years to the charming E ... E ... Evelyn, and they have two wonderful sons.'

This makes Peter and Konrad laugh a lot, because it sounds familiar.

'And,' says Konrad, 'did she come with him, this Frau Evelyn?'

'No! What a thought! She is at home, of course, minding the two wonderful sons. But what's your interest in this?'

'Yeah,' says Peter, 'what's your interest?' It doesn't seem to interest him.

'Just . . .' says Konrad.

'So, may I continue?'

Is Dad sounding a bit irritable?

'Sure,' says Konrad.

'Well, then.' Evidently, Dad has a pretty shrewd idea about what is going to happen next. When he doesn't know what is going to happen next, he's quite happy to spend time answering questions, but when he does know, he finds interruptions very annoying.

'Well,' he says again, 'the next day, the experts get a pretty good indication that not only have they found a hitherto totally unknown material, but it is one with earth-shattering properties.'

'Wow!' says Peter.

'Exactly,' says Dad. 'The next day, Franzkarl Findouter and his colleagues try to extract the crystal. They scoop the earth of the extraordinary mound carefully away from the cone of crystal, and when they finally see the top of the crystal there in front of them, then of course the first thing they think of doing is to break off a piece to use as a sample for analysis.

'But the forest snake!' says Peter, all excited.

'Exactly,' says Dad. 'The forest snake obviously wants to prevent what Professor Findouter has in mind. But now in the clear light of day, there is nothing it can do. It would be spotted immediately, and although it is big and strong, the whole research team would have no problem in overcoming and capturing it.'

'Where would they put it?' asks Peter.

'How would I know?' says Dad. 'I haven't a clue. But if five men have captured a giant snake and they are hanging onto it for dear life with all their strength, then you can be sure that one of them will think of someplace where they can shut it in. I have complete confidence in the imagination of people who have a giant wriggling snake on their hands.'

'Maybe in a suitcase,' says Konrad. He wants to get past this interruption and get on with the story.

'So anyway,' says Dad, a little crossly, 'the scientists unpack their precision tools, and among them is a little super-sharp crystal saw. They start into the crystal with it and there is this dreadful screaming sound – '

'Eeeeeee!' goes Peter.

'A sound just like that. And at last a piece of the crystal as big as your fist falls off.'

'Wow,' says Peter.

'And now,' says Dad, 'this is when the amazing thing happens. The researchers have hardly got the cut-off piece of crystal over to their measuring instruments when the hard substance suddenly turns into a soft, amorphous, utterly slimy something.'

'Eeeeeee!' shouts Peter.

'Yes! What was previously harder than stone is now suddenly softer than yoghurt. So soft that it won't even stay lying on the examination table but falls down – splat – onto the forest floor and gloops like . . . like . . . like . . .'

'Like jelly?' suggests Konrad.

'Yes! Of course. Like jelly!'

'Raspberry or lime?' Peter wants to know.

Dad explains to him that it's a simile, and that as far as this simile is concerned, flavour doesn't come into it. And now Peter is offended.

'So anyway,' says Dad. 'Now, the jelly crystal doesn't just stay on the ground. On the contrary, to the unbounded astonishment of the foregathered scientists under the leadership of Professor Franzkarl Findouter, the lump of jelly starts to creep towards the crystal.'

'Can jelly creep?' asks Peter. He still hasn't clocked what a simile is. So that he doesn't feel offended again, Konrad and Dad let on not to have heard his question at all.

'Before the eyes of the bewildered scientists,' Dad goes on, 'the transformed piece of crystal is moving faster and faster up the slope of the extraordinary mound. When it reaches the top of the crystal, it slithers back into place. And no sooner is it sitting back in its old place than it hardens again and it sticks to the rest of the substance so that you can't see any more where it was hacked off just a few minutes earlier.'

'Wow,' says Peter.

'Yes,' says Dad. 'It's unbelievable. Behaviour like this has never before been observed in any substance on earth; not in stones or in plants or in animals. Of course, things that have been cut off do occasionally grow back –'

'Like Uncle Hermann's little toe,' says Peter.

'That's right,' says Dad. 'But it never happens by itself. Not even with Uncle Hermann. No way did his toe creep to his foot and stick itself back on. In fact, Uncle Hermann and his toe had to be taken to hospital to get sewn back together again.'

Peter and Konrad remember this event well. It happened last summer. Uncle Hermann, the caretaker in Danziger Strasse, had cut off his little toe while he was cutting the grass. Two days later, he got out of hospital with a big fat bandage around his foot. From then on, he told everyone who happened to come by the whole ghastly story. And if by chance you came by more than once, you still got the whole story every time. Several weeks later, the bandage was taken off, and Konrad and Peter were allowed to look and see exactly where the toe had been sewn onto Uncle Hermann's foot. When they think of it now, they get a funny feeling in their tummies and they go very quiet.

'What's wrong?' asks Dad. 'How come you're so quiet?'

'Nothing, nothing. Go on with the story!'

'Isn't it a quarter past yet?'

'Not for ages!'

'Well,' says Dad, 'so there they stand, these important researchers. And on the one hand, there is enormous shock on their faces. But on the other hand, they are starting to get the message that the powers of this extraordinary crystal are much more extraordinary and mysterious than had previously been thought. There can be no more doubt about it. They will get the famous Nobble Prize for their research. Maybe even several Nobble Prizes. One each would be best.

So that each of them can buy half a duplex house and pay for it, money down. Ahh.' Dad stops for a moment.

'Dad,' says Konrad. 'What happens when you separate?'

'I beg your pardon?' says Dad. And – this is very unusual for him – he makes an unplanned movement and nearly gets Peter on the nose. 'What do you mean?' he asks.

'I mean, what do people do when they separate?'

'Who's getting separated?' asks Dad. He's suddenly very tense.

'A man and a woman.'

'Which man and which woman?'

'I don't know!' Now Konrad is a bit upset. 'Just . . . Or . . .' He thinks for a moment. 'Maybe Franzkarl and Evelyn Findouter.'

'They're not getting separated,' says Dad.

'But if they were?'

'They aren't.'

'Yes, but,' says Konrad, 'Imagine that they are. You can imagine anything. What happens when people separate?'

'What happens!' says Dad. 'What happens!' How should he know? And anyway, Dad does not want to imagine that a prospective Nobble Prizewinner is separating from the mother of his wonderful sons.

'Please,' says Konrad. And then he says the magic words that Mum sometimes uses: 'For my sake, okay?'

'Well,' says Dad. 'What happens when people separate? Probably the two people don't love each other any more. They're always fighting and so they just separate. The wife stays on in the house, the husband gets himself a little flat and then they go to court to decide who gets how much of their joint money, and who gets to keep what furniture. And that's it.'

'But if they have children.'

'What about it?'

'Can you get separated even if you have children?'

Dad goes: 'Hrrmph!' Then he says, 'Yes. You can get separated even if you have children. Where did you hear about it?'

'About what?'

'About this separation business.'

'Just,' says Konrad.

That seems to satisfy Dad. On the evening of a day where he goes to the bank in the afternoon to have them calculate his mortgage payments, he's probably happy if at least there are no major problems with the serial story. He tells a bit more about the astonishment of the researchers and then they all have a think about what the researchers might do to stop the jelly crystal from creeping away. None of them can come up with a solution, and at exactly a quarter past eight, Dad gives the two boys a goodnight kiss.

This evening, Konrad goes straight to his own bed. Apparently the two mice have nothing to discuss. Peter seems to fall asleep immediately, but Konrad lies awake for some time. He can hear his parents talking downstairs in the living room. He can't make out what they are saying. But they're not fighting anyway. And when he is quite sure about that, Konrad falls asleep.

Crazy Bugs 3

It's arrived. Tuesday. Not any old Tuesday, but the Tuesday on which Konrad Bantelmann – future fifth class pupil, inhabitant of number 17a, passionate Lego player and owner of a very intelligent list – is to meet a girl. A girl who possesses *Crazy Bugs 3* but unfortunately also a repulsive rabbit, and whose parents are very sadly separated. How can that be?

Konrad spends the whole morning playing Lego, but no matter what he makes – missile rockets, space stations or transporters – nothing goes right. Somehow, everything manages to look like a rabbit hutch.

The time is fast approaching. All Konrad has to do is take his eyes off the time, and suddenly at least half an hour has passed. Just to make sure, Konrad goes down to the kitchen a couple of times to check, but the clock down there is racing away like mad and it's lunchtime already. What a day!

And for lunch, there's spinach. It's not that Konrad doesn't like spinach. Spinach is good. Or, more precisely, spinach is not bad. But unfortunately it is extremely difficult to eat a plate of spinach in such a way that all the spinach is inside the person and none of it ends up somewhere else. The spinach won't hear of it. Spinach wants to get everywhere: on the table, on your sweatshirt sleeves, on your trousers and especially on your face, just next to your ear. Why spinach wants to do this is unknown. But spinach must want to do it pretty badly, because although Konrad has been trying very hard for years, the spinach manages every time to find its favourite places to settle. Which inevitably leads to Mum-panic.

Now, Konrad could point out that in the case of his brother Peter, spinach manages to reach much more remote places, for example, the top of his head and under his feet, from where it could spread itself all over the house. But if he mentions this, Konrad does not make himself popular, because then he's told that he is older, and should know better, and moreover he should be showing a good example to his younger brother. That's just the way it is. So, Konrad takes up the spinach challenge once again. As a precautionary measure, he bends so far over his plate that there is at the most five millimetres between the spinach and his mouth. That looks good, but even within this space of five millimetres, the spinach is sure to be able to make a dash for it.

All's well at first, but then a siren suddenly starts up outside on Hedwig Dransfeld Strasse. Is it the fire brigade? Could one of the new duplexes have gone on fire? And if so, which one? Maybe one where a child who's on Konrad's list lives? Maybe it's number 28b?

Quick, to the window for a look! Peter has the same idea at the same time, and as the two of them leap up from the table at the same moment, their shoulders collide and there is such a tussle that Konrad's fork, which he had put down a bit crooked at the edge of his plate, unfortunately slips to one side. Being somewhat overloaded, it falls from the table and hits off the side of the chair, which creates a catapult effect. This catapult effect causes a forkload of spinach to fly through the air and to land – splat – against the dining-room wall. Not until then does the fork clatter to the floor.

Major Mum-panic sets in. Peter starts up a precautionary wail, and – wouldn't you know it? – the noise outside turns out not to be the fire brigade after all but a car alarm, and there is nothing to be seen except the man from number 18b, who keeps pulling a cable out from under the bonnet of his car until the siren finally stops. That's the end of lunch.

Mum scrapes the spinach off the wall and says horrid things about her sons. The boys excuse themselves and go to their rooms and think dark thoughts about spinach, while their mice, Lackilug and Mattchoo, go so far as to suggest what might be done about eliminating spinach altogether from the world. Just as well no one else understands what they are saying.

And then all of a sudden it's a quarter to two! Which means that Konrad had better be on his way, because he has to meet a girl called Fridz with a d and very likely also her horrible rabbit. So he goes downstairs, puts on his shoes and calls out as usual, 'Bye. I'm not going far.' Just as he has his hand on the door handle, his mother calls him back. Mum-panic is still in evidence.

'Stay right there! You are under house arrest.'

'I beg your pardon?' says Konrad.

Fine, anyone can understand 'stay right there'. But what

in the world does 'house arrest' mean? Konrad Bantelmann doesn't know what 'house arrest' means. And he says so.

'What's house arrest?'

So there they stand, Mum Bantelmann and her son Konrad, who still has his hand on the door handle. And while Konrad goes on thinking about the words 'house arrest,' it has dawned on Mum that she's done something wrong. Because while of course it is unacceptable for the boys to spread spinach on the newly painted walls of the recently built number 17a, on the other hand, a phrase like 'house arrest' is just as out of place in Hedwig Dransfeld Strasse as spinach on the walls. That is a phrase out of the Dark Ages, when parents locked their children up in their rooms for the slightest thing. House arrest hadn't existed even when Mum was called Edith and was a little girl. Even then house arrest had been abolished – and now many, many years later, at a time when her son Konrad doesn't even know what house arrest means, she, a thoroughly modern Dransfeld mother, is planning to impose such an old-fashioned punishment! And all because of a spot of spinach! Mum flushes a little. But just as she is about to answer, it finally occurs to Konrad what 'house arrest' must mean.

'Arrest', that's what a policeman threatens a robber with in one of his books, and it means something like jail. So, Mum wants to turn the house into a jail for him, which in turn means that he, Konrad Bantelmann, has the best excuse in the whole world not to turn up to his appointment with this Fridz. What a piece of luck, thinks Konrad, and on a day like today! He vows never to think badly of spinach again. Hurray!

Konrad does not, of course, say 'Hurray!' Instead, he makes a gesture that means roughly, 'Oh well, that's life.' And he says aloud, 'I'll just go back upstairs then.' That is to say, he doesn't say it really loudly, but rather softly, so that it sounds half-sad and half-sulky.

'No, no!' says Mum quickly. 'I didn't mean it like that.'

What's that supposed to mean? Did she intend 'house arrest' to mean something different? And if so, what?

'You can go,' says Mum. 'You have an appointment. We'll discuss the spinach this evening.'

There he stands, then, Konrad Bantelmann. No such luck after all. What can he say? Should he ask for a spot of house arrest so that he doesn't have to visit the wretched rabbit? No, that would never do.

Instead, he mumbles 'Thanks,' as quietly as possible, opens the door a crack and squeezes out. There's no way back now. What had Mum said yesterday? He'd just have to go through it.

Konrad walks slowly along Hedwig Dransfeld Strasse, his eyes glued to the ground, to the new paving stones, which are still quite bare, without a single piece of trodden-on chewing gum on them. Just as long as he doesn't meet anyone. As long as no one speaks to him. So that the whole of The Dransfeld doesn't start gossiping about how he has a date with a girl.

Outside number 28b Konrad looks up for the first time. He can't see anyone, but that doesn't mean that no one has seen him. In 27b, for example, the twins, Lena and Lisa, could be watching him from behind a flowery net curtain or a china goose. But Konrad has an idea. He knows a trick. He got it out of a detective story. He takes a euro coin out of his pocket, keeping his fist closed over it, then he bends over and gropes on the ground. And when he straightens up, he has the coin in his hand, so that anyone watching would be sure to think he'd just found it on the ground. That's part one of the clever trick. Now for the second part. Konrad looks pointedly left and right as if to say, who could have lost this coin? Who could it be? And the third part of the trick: Konrad looks up the drive of number 28b and smacks himself with the flat of his hand on the forehead, the way Mum does when she finally remembers, after many hours, where she has put her keys. That's supposed to mean, obviously it's the people in number 28b who have lost the coin. The fourth part of the trick goes like this: Konrad holds the coin up as high as possible, he goes to the door of number 28b and he rings the doorbell. Nobody on earth could possibly conclude after all this that Konrad Bantelmann is ringing the doorbell because he is supposed to meet a girl.

'Hi,' says Fridz.

'Hi,' says Konrad.

'Come in!' She grabs Konrad's sweatshirt and drags him into the house. That's girls for you.

'There's no admission charge,' she says.

Konrad, of course, still has the coin in his raised hand.

'Oh,' he says, 'this is – ah – for the rabbit.'

'Great,' says Fridz, 'thank you very much. But he doesn't eat money.'

Yeah, very funny. This Fridz is by far the sharpest-tongued girl that Konrad has ever met. But he won't let himself be beaten as easily as that.

'I know,' he says. 'But I thought you should buy him a fresh lettuce.'

As a smart answer, that's pretty good. Except that now the rabbit is the centre of attention again. And that was exactly what Konrad wanted to avoid.

But Konrad's luck is very changeable today. Fridz takes the coin from him, and says, 'Shut up about the rabbit. Just take your shoes off and come upstairs. I'm playing *Crazy Bugs* and I've got to level two already.'

'Cool,' says Konrad.

Half an hour later, they are both on level five, and Konrad is laughing so hard that the tears are running down his cheeks. Because firstly, this game really is very funny, and secondly, Fridz can be really sharp about what's happening, and funny too. If she doesn't stop soon, Konrad is going to explode. His stomach hurts from laughing.

'Ahh!' she says now. 'Just you wait, you evil spawn of blue-spotted horse-poo flies! I'm going to mash you into brown horse-pooh mush.' With that, she makes the little man on the screen race around like mad with his fly-swatter. But instead of catching a single bug, he knocks the dishes off a little table, the flowers off the windowsill and the pictures off the walls. In the end, he even knocks a hole in the window, through which more and more and yet more insects come pouring into the virtual room. Konrad can hardly breathe, he is laughing so hard. Sebastian from number 9a, who would quite happily play *Crazy Bugs 2* all day, takes the game completely seriously. The first time they sat together at the computer and Konrad let a few bugs go that he could easily have caught on level two, Sebastian got really cross with him. 'I'll never get to level five if I play with you,' he'd said.

But Fridz is unbelievably expert at *Crazy Bugs 3*. They'd got to level five in no time, but then Fridz had suddenly started messing about. Of course, their lovely level five score was in ruins within seconds, because the new bugs immediately free the ones Konrad and Fridz had just captured, and then the whole lot start swarming all over the little man, who's screeching like mad now and scratching himself. The bug-counter on the left of the screen is rattling away downwards at a great rate towards zero, until finally the signs light up that tell you you are the lousiest bug-catcher under the sun. And the computer laughs wickedly.

'That's that!' cries Fridz. 'So what'll we do now?'

'Play mothers and fathers?' says Konrad.

'Oh no! How on earth did he let that out? It must have to do with the mood of hilarity Fridz has created with her smart remarks and all her fooling about at the computer.

Mothers and fathers, of all things! Because that's every girl's favourite thing to play. And of all the utterly embarrassing games on earth, this one is the most embarrassing. What's he going to do now, if Fridz says, 'Super'? But that is not what she says at all. Instead, she suddenly goes all serious. 'Nah,' she says. 'We don't play that game any more around here.'

Oh, of course! Konrad wishes the earth would open and swallow him up. Fridz's parents are separated! That was the loopiest suggestion he could possibly have made. He mumbles something that might, at a stretch, be interpreted as 'sorry'. It had been such good fun until now. Hopefully Fridz isn't offended.

'It's okay,' she says. And then she gives Konrad such a cheeky look. 'Do you play mothers and fathers at home?'

Konrad smacks himself on the forehead. No way!

'And your parents,' says Fridz, 'they're still together?'

'Sure they are!'

'Nothing sure about it.' Fridz taps a few keys and *Crazy Bugs 3* disappears from the screen. 'Nothing is sure. My mum and dad are separated. My real Uncle Klaus and my real Aunt Sabine are actually divorced. And my pretend Uncle Jürgen and my pretend Aunt Marie too.'

'Wow,' says Konrad. He can't think of anything else to say.

'Yeah,' says Fridz. 'And Paul and Elvira, whom I don't call uncle and aunt, they've decided that they want to try living in separate apartments for a year.'

'Oh,' says Konrad. 'And your dad? Where does he live now?'

Fridz turns the computer off. 'With Kristine. Kristine with a K. Imagine! With a K at the beginning. Like kindergarten. Or kick.'

'And who is this Kristine?'

'Dad's girlfriend. Just think, she has short blonde hair.' Fridz demonstrates with two fingers. 'This short. You wouldn't believe it. It only takes her ten minutes to wash her hair. Ten minutes, including drying and everything. When Mum washes her hair, it takes half the afternoon. And if she puts colour in too, then that's the whole evening gone.'

'I see,' says Konrad. This is extraordinary information. Fridz's mother's red hair is dyed and Fridz's father lives with a girlfriend called Kristine with a K. And on top of that, all Fridz's relations are divorced. Konrad must seem like a person who has no proper experience of life. He feels somehow rather small. And because nobody likes feeling small, he tries hard to think what kind of catastrophe he can offer to match Fridz's experience.

Right enough, there is something! And so Konrad explains at great and elaborate length how he and his disgusting brother had catapulted half a bowl of spinach at the wall. What? Half a bowl? No, of course it was a whole bowl. And the spinach had spattered as high as the ceiling. And the bowl smashed into a thousand pieces. And what a rant Mum went on! And, and, and – Konrad does wonder if maybe he's telling lies. Not really. Life, Dad always says, is full of the beginnings of stories. You just have to think up a good ending for them. And besides, Fridz is roaring with laughter. And that's worth a bit of fibbing, isn't it?

At the Canal

'Let's go to the canal,' says Fridz, when she is able to talk again.

To the canal! What should he say to that? Going to the canal has not, so far, been discussed in the Bantelmann house. There's no need, because Konrad is the kind of child who has an inbuilt sense of what is forbidden. Konrad always knows in advance perfectly well what he is not allowed to do. The lovely lawn in the park? *Keep off the grass.* The funny stuffed animal in the natural history museum? *Do not touch.* And the interesting little path along by the railway tracks? *No entry.*

It was the same with the canal. Konrad only had to see it from afar, that time when the houses in The Dransfeld were being built – and he knew at once that you weren't allowed to go there. And most certainly not alone.

'Ah,' he says now, 'to the canal?'

Of course, that is not meant to sound like 'Oh no, no! That's not allowed!' It's meant to sound more like, 'But would that be cool?'

Fridz either has no ear for such subtleties, or she's worked out what Konrad really meant to say.

'Do you not dare, or are you just not allowed?'

Both: Konrad doesn't dare to say that he is probably not allowed to go to the canal. He adds quickly, 'Of course I dare.' This, on the one hand, is not exactly true, but on the other hand it's the only thing that he dares to say. Life can be difficult.

'Let's go, then,' says Fridz. She grabs Konrad by the arm and pulls him down into the hall. She yanks her shoes out of a rickety little cupboard and calls out, 'Bye, Henri, we're just going to the ca-na-al!'

Who on earth is this Henri? Konrad wonders.

'My mum,' says Fridz, as if he had actually asked the question.

'Excuse me?'

Fridz has one shoe on already and Konrad hasn't even picked his up yet.

'My mum's name is Henriette. But Dad always calls her Henri.'

Oh boy! Everything is so weird in number 28b. Konrad tries to imagine Dad calling Mum Eddi. He finally finds his shoes.

'Bye, Henri!' calls Fridz again.

But there's no answer.

'Maybe your mum's out.'

'Nah. She's not out, she's here.' All at once, Fridz looks serious again. She even has a big frown in the middle of her forehead.

'Keep quiet!' she says.

Konrad would have to stop breathing to be any quieter. He does so, carefully.

'I can't hear a thing.'

'Me neither.' Konrad breathes again, and it's not a moment too soon.

'Henri!' Fridz shouts loudly.

Silence.

'Hell!' says Fridz. She throws the second shoe at the front door. With a bound she is up the stairs again.

Konrad hears her calling 'Mum! Mum! Where are you?'

What's going on? And what should Konrad do now? Stand here like the town clock? Or slither off home? Maybe something bad has happened. Or at least something that he shouldn't be around for. But what?

Very slowly, Konrad goes to the staircase and starts climbing. From there he can hear doors being slammed, and Fridz's excited voice. And finally he sees what's wrong. At least, he doesn't exactly see what's wrong. He only sees that Fridz's mum is lying, fully dressed, on the bed in the master bedroom, and that Fridz is bending over her. Her mum appears to be asleep and Fridz is trying to wake her up. She's screaming at her mum and she's shaking her. And now, yes, now she's even slapping her across the face. So hard that you can hear the smack.

'Mum!' she keeps calling. 'Wake up, Mum!' But her mum seems to be sleeping so deeply that she is totally out of it.

'Quick, help me!' Fridz calls out and runs past Konrad into the bathroom, where she chucks the toothbrushes out of the tooth glasses and fills one of them with water.

'You fill the other one,' she says and she's gone.

'Quick!' she calls again.

Konrad hurries. As he comes back into the bedroom with the full tooth glass, he sees Fridz pouring the water over her mother's face. Without thinking, he passes her his glass, she takes it and does the same thing again.

'Hey,' says her mother then, very softly. Her face and hair are wet and so is half the bed.

'Hey,' she says again. 'What are you doing?'

Then she pushes her wet hair off her face.

Fridz is standing by the bed. She says nothing.

'I was asleep,' says her mother. At last she notices Konrad. 'Oh, it's you,' she says. 'She does such nice things, Friederike, doesn't she? You'd think she was nuts, the little one.'

She's sitting up now, and she tries to pull Fridz towards her but Fridz pulls herself free.

'We're going to the canal,' she says bluntly. 'I just wanted to let you know.' And then she takes Konrad by the arm and pulls him out of the room.

'Be careful of the water!' her mother calls after them.

Half an hour later, Fridz and Konrad are at the canal. They let their legs hang over the steep bank and Fridz is throwing stones, one after another, into the dark water. Neither of them has said anything yet. Not even when a long, flat boat went by lying so low in the water that you'd think it was going to go under.

Konrad has been thinking hard. Maybe Fridz is slightly mad after all? Maybe her mum is sick? Or is it just that things between Fridz and her mum are very different from how things are at home? Hard to say.

He takes a look at Fridz out of the corner of his eye, the

way she's throwing stones in the canal, her teeth tightly clamped together. If she keeps this up, it will soon be so full of stones that the water will be all dammed up and the next boat will run aground.

One thing is sure, thinks Konrad at last: she's not really crazy. At any rate, he doesn't want her to be crazy. Because although she does such very odd things, he still thinks she's nice. Or maybe it's precisely because she does such odd things that he thinks she's nice.

At last, he dares to ask, 'What was all that about? You know, with your mother?'

Fridz looks at him. 'She was sleeping again,' she says.

'Yes, well, I know that, but why did you throw water in her face?'

'To wake her up.'

'Right,' says Konrad. She's being pretty snippy. And he doesn't want to ask any more, because he's afraid that snippy could easily turn into downright nasty. In the end, though, he does ask, 'But why did she have to wake up?'

First Fridz throws a whole handful of stones into the water. 'You really haven't a clue, have you?' she says. 'My mum is unhappy, do you see? And because she is unhappy, she can't always manage. Then she just goes to bed and sleeps. She can bear it all a bit better while she is asleep. Or so she says.'

'So just let her sleep, then.'

But Fridz shakes her head, making her long red hair fly about. 'She takes tablets,' she says. 'Because she can't sleep without them. But – ' and here she boxes Konrad pretty hard in the arm, 'these tablets, I'm telling you, if you take too many of them, they're dangerous.'

'Ah,' says Konrad. 'So could a person sleep until next Sunday?'

'Oh, you thicko! You don't sleep. You die!'

'Oh, right, I see,' says Konrad.

And then the two of them sit by the dark brown canal without speaking. Until Fridz says, 'I could kill her!'

'Who?' cries Konrad, shocked. 'Your mum?'

'Don't talk such rubbish!' Fridz stands up and starts walking, and Konrad has to hurry to catch up with her.

'That Kristine,' says Fridz. 'Kristine with a K. My dad's girlfriend. I could kill her. If it wasn't for her, then we wouldn't have all this trouble. The stupid cow.'

'Hmm,' says Konrad. 'You should tell your dad to come home. Tell him he should do it for your mum's sake. That usually works.'

'You are soft in the head.' Fridz doesn't even look at Konrad. She just walks more quickly along the canal path. 'What do you think he would do if I said that?'

'Dunno,' says Konrad, who is a little out of breath.

Then Fridz stops. She stands in front of Konrad with her hands on her hips. 'My dear child,' she says in a very deep voice. 'I know that all this is hard for you. But there is nothing I can do about that. You see, my angel, when two people don't love each other any more, then they have to separate. Otherwise, it all just gets even worse. And that's no good to anyone. So!'

'So,' says Fridz again, this time in her normal voice. 'And

then he hugs me and gives me a cuddle and says, "You're my little dandelion, my little princess, my fairy queen." She rolls her eyes. 'And then off he goes again to his blonde Kristine.'

Oh dear, oh dear! Konrad senses danger. Fridz looks as if she is about to burst into tears. And then Konrad Bantelmann would be here at the canal, which is not allowed, he would be here with a girl, which is just not right for a boy, and the girl would, moreover, be crying! Konrad just couldn't cope with so many terrible and forbidden things all at once.

'Well,' he says quickly. 'Well . . .' He has to say something that will make sure Fridz doesn't start crying. 'You could . . .' he says, though he still has no idea what on earth she could do. 'You could...set a trap for Kristine!'

'What kind of a trap?'

Well, at least she's not crying.

'A trap . . . with . . . a trap with . . . '

Oh lordy me, Konrad Bantelmann, you are getting absolutely nowhere. He can't think of a thing to say. What on earth made him suggest a trap? It's a cracked idea. 'With insects!'

'Huh?' says Fridz.

'An insect trap,' says Konrad. 'Like in the game. Level two. She could fall into it and then she'd have to scratch herself all over.'

He knew it was a ridiculous idea.

'Hmm,' says Fridz, crinkling up her eyes and peering at Konrad.

Now what?

'Ye-es,' says Fridz. She says it the way gangsters do in those films that Konrad isn't supposed to watch.

'Yes,' she says again. 'That's brilliant. We'll set a rabbit trap for the stupid cow.'

A rabbit trap? Was she serious?

'Super!' cries Fridz. 'Su-per!' She is thrilled. 'That's a super idea. We'll send Dad's last Flemish Giant to her.' She punches Konrad in the chest. 'Don't you get it?'

Konrad doesn't get anything.

'Yahooey,' says Fridz. 'The stupid cow is allergic to rabbits. That's why Dad has to keep the beasts away from her.'

Boy, has he struck it lucky!

Or maybe not.

'Yes, allergic.' Fridz is so delighted that she starts to dance. 'The silly goose! She's allergic to fur. She only needs to go *near* a rabbit and she starts to sneeze and to sweat. And her throat swells up and her hands go red!'

'And her hair goes purple!' says Konrad.

'Yes.' Fridz whispers into Konrad's ear. 'Her teeth too, and her fingernails!'

'And she gets green spots on her stomach!'

'And her earlobes go yellow. And her toenails curl up. And her knees turn to jelly. And her head too.'

Fridz is jumping with joy. Suddenly she grabs Konrad by both arms, pulls him towards her and gives him a kiss on the cheek. The kiss almost hurts.

'Right,' she says and looks into his eyes. 'Let's go! Whoever thinks up the worst thing wins.'

And off they go. It's a good game. A wonderful game. You

wouldn't believe how many good ideas you get when you've decided to be good and mean.

Of course, Fridz wins. It's unbelievable the things she thinks up. She is beside herself with delight.

When they get to number 28b, she puts her hand over Konrad's mouth.

'Not a word,' she says, 'till tomorrow! We'll do it tomorrow, right? Straight after breakfast.'

'Right,' says Konrad.

'And don't breathe a word to a soul! Deal?'

'Deal.'

'Good. I have to go in now and see to Henri.'

Fridz waves and disappears into the house.

Konrad waves back. Then he makes his way slowly home, thinking the whole thing over. He had a date with a girl. He'd experienced something pretty awful. He'd been to the canal, where he isn't allowed to go. He'd thought of something mean. And . . . he'd been kissed!

Konrad remembers his Dransfeld list. He should really write all this up. Oh – think about something else, quick!

It works. Sort of.

Kristine Crisis

At dinner that evening in the Bantelmanns' house, the thing that Konrad has been dreading doesn't happen. To his great surprise, nobody mentions spinach, neither its flight nor its landing. And there is nothing to be seen on the wall. Mum has painted over the mark and dried it off with the hairdryer.

However, there is a demand for freshly squeezed Konrad. They want to squeeze words out of him, the way you squeeze juice out of a lemon. After all, he's just had his first date with a girl. His parents are all agog.

Konrad is not, however, a lemon, and he is not going to let anyone squeeze him. But he does not say, 'I'm telling you nothing!' That would be stupid. Instead, he puts up passive resistance.

How did it go? he is asked.

'Well,' is the expansive answer.

And what had they done?

'Played.'

Good heavens! How extraordinary! And what exactly had they played?

'Different things.'

My goodness, what a talkative boy!

Mum and Dad Bantelmann are starting to get a bit edgy. Could he maybe be a little bit more precise? Please? Please!

'*Crazy Bugs 3*,' says Konrad cheerfully.

And then at last comes the question that he had been most afraid of. What's Friederike's family like?

'Nice,' says Konrad stoutly.

Then Dad gets up from his chair and comes and kneels on the floor beside Konrad.

'Mercy, O great master,' he says in a tearful voice. 'Would the great master please grant us the favour of letting us in just a little bit on the adventures that have befallen him this afternoon on his voyage of discovery into deepest Dransfeld? For we, the humble and loyal Wolfgang and Edith Bantelmann, have been entrusted with the upbringing of the lord and merciful master Konrad, and therefore we have, in this regard, a natural interest in knowing where our silent hero has been tootling around.'

Peter doesn't understand a word of this, but he laughs a lot anyway, putting his chocolate in mortal danger.

'Watch out!' shouts Mum.

She means Peter and his drinking chocolate. But the warning applies to Konrad too. Because if he doesn't tell them something, then his parents will be cross. On the other hand, he must not tell them anything, because if he says anything, he is sure to let slip the dreadful tale of the sleeping mother and her tablets. And that must not happen! Konrad is absolutely sure that it would be either forbidden or stupid to tell about that. Maybe even both. So, in order to avoid these two dangers, he tells in great detail all about how they got to level five in *Crazy Bugs 3* and how Fridz then went totally berserk and chased the little bug-catcher around the screen and how the window got broken and how the other bugs then – '

'Thank you,' says Dad. He's back on his chair again now. 'Thank you very much,' he says again. But it doesn't sound altogether friendly. 'Many thanks for the helpful information,' he says, but then Mum makes some kind of a signal to him and the rest of dinner proceeds quietly and uneventfully. To everyone's surprise, even Peter's chocolate survives.

Just two hours later, Dad is lying on Peter's bed and the boys are trying, for the nth time, not to kick him in the stomach, or anywhere else, while trying to get their legs into the most comfortable position.

'Well, then,' says Dad. 'Anabasis the forest snake. The mysterious crystal. The learned Franzkarl Findouter. And . . . the treacherous Dr Bigomil A. Deceiver.' He seems to be trying to recall the story bit by bit and with considerable effort. Then he suddenly finds the thread that holds all these parts of the story together.

'Right,' he says. 'Right. We've heard about the secret powers of the crystal and, ehh, we can guess that the scientists are going to find it very difficult to get it quickly and safely to a great laboratory.'

'Dad,' says Konrad.

'Yes?' It's not easy to tell whether or not Dad is receptive to interruptions today.

'Dad,' says Konrad again. 'This Findouter . . . '

'Yes, what about him?'

'He *is* divorced.'

'What?' says Dad, sounding neither entirely pleased nor

extremely irritated. Just a bit surprised.

'Yes,' says Konrad. 'I'm sure of it now. But he hasn't got two sons. He has a daughter. She's called . . . ehh . . . ' Konrad pauses, but after two or three more 'ehhs' he says quickly, 'She's called Luise.'

'I see. And how do you know all this?'

Hmm, how does he know this? Usually, only Dad knows how the stories go, and Konrad and Peter just ask the questions. So Dad has every right to be surprised.

'I just do,' says Konrad.

Not much of an answer. And as you might expect, Dad is not very happy with it.

'What does that mean, you just know?'

It's all down to Konrad now. If he says 'I just do' again, then the forest snake story will probably continue the way Dad wants it to go. But if he can think up some reason why Franzkarl Findouter is divorced, then Dad would have to bring it into the story. And that's important for Konrad. Very important, in fact.

'I know it because of the mobile,' he says. 'When you're away, you ring up every evening on your mobile. But this Findouter is on an expedition in the jungle, and he hasn't rung home a single time.'

'Hmm,' says Dad. 'Hasn't rung home? Not even once?'

'No. You never said he did.'

'Hmm,' says Dad again. It's true, he keeps ringing home himself. Last week, he'd even got a new mobile so he could do it, one that you can fold up so that it fits nicely in your pocket.

'So what do you think?' he says after a while. 'Has he got another woman?'

'Yes,' says Konrad. 'Another woman. A girlfriend.'

'Right, I see,' says Dad slowly. 'And what is this other woman called?'

'Kristine,' says Konrad quickly. 'Kristine with a K.'

'And what's her other name?'

Her other name? How on earth should Konrad know!

'How about Kristine Crisis?' says Dad.

Peter, who has been lying there, struck dumb with astonishment, suddenly laughs out loud.

'Kristine Crisis! Kristine Crisis!' he shouts and kicks out all around him.

It's not entirely clear if he knows what a crisis is. But just as Konrad always knows in advance what is not allowed, Peter has a pretty good nose for what is funny.

Well, thinks Konrad, it might do.

And so it does.

'OK – she's called Kristine Crisis,' says Dad. 'Or more precisely, Dr Kristine Crisis. She is, let's say, twenty-nine years old, and she wrote her doctoral thesis on mysterious zig-zag footprints in Scottish wheatfields. After that, she became Franzkarl Findouter's personal assistant, and they fell in love on an expedition to the temples of the Minka. Are you happy now?'

'Yes,' says Konrad.

'So I can go on with the story?'

'No,' says Konrad.

'What do you mean, no?'

'We have to tell the whole thing. And that means more about Luise.'

'Who is Luise?'

'I told you,' says Konrad, in a reproachful tone, 'that's the daughter of Franzkarl and Evelyn Findouter. She's at home with her mum. And her mum is not well.'

'Oh, no,' says Dad. 'I have to tell all about this?'

'Yes,' says Konrad curtly. It sounds like an order.

'No,' says Peter. 'You have to tell about the forest snake. And about Dr Deceiver's crystal.'

There are days when you would like to roast your little brother over an open fire. You can't, of course. You'd probably regret it later. But Konrad would very much like to at least pinch Peter in the leg to make him shut up. But he can't do that either, because Dad is stretched out between the two of them. So what can he do? And then it strikes him. He looks over Dad's body at Peter and says just one word: 'Spinach.'

It works! Because if Konrad tells about the flying spinach, then not only he but also Peter will have to hear the lecture that Dad will be obliged to give. So Peter doesn't say another word. But that only makes Dad curious about the secret communication between his sons.

'Let's get on with it,' he says loudly and as if he hasn't noticed a thing. 'So where do they live, this Frau Findouter and her daughter Luise?'

'In a very new house,' says Konrad. 'In a very new house among lots of other new houses.'

'Aha,' says Dad. 'And Professor Findouter?'

'He didn't move in at all.'

'Hah! So where does he live then?'

'He lives with Kristine Crisis.'

'I see,' says Dad. 'So that's the way it is. Things are in a bad way. This is one of those unhappy situations into which even the happiest family can slip. And as is often the case, it has affected the little daughter Luise most of all.'

'No,' Konrad interrupts. 'It's worse for the mother.'

'How do you mean?'

But Konrad only shakes his head. Dad has to tell it himself.

'So, the mother is in a bad way,' says Dad slowly. He has to think his way into the story. 'But it's no wonder,' he continues. 'For nearly two years, she has had to make all the decisions about the new house all by herself. She's had to choose the tiles for the bathroom and the carpet for Luise's bedroom while her famous husband was in the jungle, digging for bits of pottery. But she did it gladly. Because do you know what she thought?'

Konrad shakes his head again.

'She thought, when we've moved into the lovely new house, then Professor Findouter will feel so at ease there that he will immediately start looking for things to research that are not in the back of beyond. On the contrary, he will be a home-based researcher, and he can come home every evening to his wife and daughter, and he can stay home altogether at the weekend. Is that the way it was?' asks Dad.

Konrad nods.

'Good,' says Dad. 'But unfortunately, it all turns out totally differently. When the Findouters' new house is almost ready, and Frau Findouter has organised the move, the professor is just up a Minka pyramid in the temple city of Hattumaku.'

Peter laughs at 'Hattumaku.'

'Exactly,' says Konrad. Once again he threatens, 'spinach,' and Peter goes quiet.

'It's evening in Hattumaku', says Dad. He seems to be getting gradually interested in the new story. 'The sun is going down, blood red, over the Minka temples, and Franzkarl Findouter suddenly feels desperately lonely. He'd much prefer to be at home with his wife and daughter than sitting here on this damned pile of stones. They could be cooking a barbecue or going on a cycle or just sitting by the canal, watching the boats. But it cannot be. Things have to be researched in foreign lands, so that later, fat books can be written and new bits of pottery can be put on display in museums.'

'And then?'

'Hmm, well, as the professor is sitting there sadly on his pyramid, gawping at the sunset, who should come by with a sausage in one hand and a bottle of cold beer in the other?'

'Crisis,' says Konrad darkly.

'Exactly. Dr Crisis, who takes very good care of her dear professor, comes prancing up the wobbly old stones, waving the sausage and the beer bottle in the air while she is still quite far off and calling in a sweet voice – well, what do you think she is calling?'

'Dinner is ready,' says Konrad.

'Wrong,' says Dad. 'Sweetly, she calls –'

'She calls "sweetie"?'

'No! She calls in a sweet voice.'

'"Come on. Here's something yummy," says Konrad. It sounds bittersweet.

'Right,' says Dad. 'And what do you think happens when dear little Kristine presses the sausage and the beer into Findouter's hand?'

'He gobbles it all up,' says Konrad. 'What else would he do?'

'And what next?'

'Dunno!'

'Well, the professor falls head over heels in love with his enchanting assistant. Ping!'

'Just like that?' says Konrad. 'Ping? Just because of the sausage and the beer?'

'No,' says Dad. 'Not just because of the sausage and the beer. But just at that moment, Herr Findouter has a deep need for tender loving care. And because his wife, who is in charge of the tender loving care department, is not there, then he transfers his need to the good Fräulein Crisis.'

'I don't think so,' says Konrad. 'What does he do then?'

'Well,' says Dad, 'what does he do? He does what people do in cases like this. He eats his sausage, drinks his beer, wipes his mouth, sits his Fräulein Crisis down beside him, and then the two of them watch together as the sun goes down over the old temples. He puts his arm around her shoulders, and whispers some very nice things into her ear.'

To show exactly what he means, Dad puts an arm around

Peter and whispers something into his ear. It tickles like mad, which makes Peter laugh and kick Dad in the stomach.

'Ooof,' says Dad.

'And then?' Konrad is much more curious now than he ever was about the forest snake story.

But Dad is pinching and tickling Peter.

'And then?' says Konrad again.

'Hmm.' Dad lets Peter go again. 'Well, it depends.'

'On what?'

'On Fräulein Crisis. If she moves a bit away, or if she lets out a piercing scream or if she smacks him smartly on the hand, then... well, then, the lonely Findouter will go into his tent, drink maybe another seven bottles of beer, fall asleep and tomorrow he will have a headache. But on the other hand...'

Dad pauses. He seems to be thinking.

Konrad is very quiet.

'If, on the other hand, Fräulein Crisis sits tight and listens to what he whispers in her ear, and lets out just a soft 'Oh' and a 'Yes, of course' or even if she cuddles in closer to him and lays her head on his shoulder...'

Dad goes back to messing about with Peter.

'Then unhappiness will take its course,' Dad concludes.

'How come?'

'Ah,' says Dad. 'Because then the professor will be happy. So terribly happy that all he wants to do for the rest of his life is to sit on a pyramid beside his Fräulein Crisis and murmur nice things into her ear. He wants that so much that everything about his wife and his daughter and his new house becomes unimportant. And before the sun has disappeared behind the pyramids, he has decided not to move into the new house, but instead to leave his wife and child and to live with his Fräulein Crisis in a two-person tent. '

'And to sleep with her,' says Konrad.

'I beg your pardon!' says Dad. He sounds pretty shocked. He did explain to his son Konrad Bantelmann a few months ago that people who love each other sleep together. But even so, he is always shocked when he realises that Konrad has remembered this and possibly even understood it.

'Yes, of course,' he says quickly. 'Of course they will sleep with each other. Like man and wife.'

Konrad groans. 'And of course, they'll have children.'

'Possibly,' says Dad. 'Possibly they will have children.'

Then he looks at the clock. It is exactly a quarter past eight. He looks at his boys. They are lying very quietly, and they look pretty tired. So he gives each of them a goodnight kiss, and, most unusually, he picks up Konrad, who is far too big for this sort of thing, and carries him to his own bed.

Then he goes downstairs into the living room. Konrad can hear his parents talking down there. They are speaking very quietly, as they always do when their sons must under no circumstances understand what they are saying. And no matter how hard Konrad tries, he doesn't understand a single word. And so he goes to sleep.

Seriously Flemish Giant

The next morning just after breakfast, Konrad sets off for number 28b, feeling a little anxious. The anxiety is sitting roughly at the level of his navel and it grows with every step he takes, until it has become a giant worry. Was this dippy Friederike really serious about that idea of hers – setting a rabbit trap for her father's girlfriend?

Konrad doesn't like this idea one little bit. Yesterday, when they'd been imagining all the things that were going to happen to this Kristine when her rabbit allergy broke out, he hadn't for a moment thought that they would really send a rabbit to the poor woman. You just say stuff like that. You do it every day. But you don't actually do half of what you say. Konrad thinks of all the mischief they plan at school during break – pitching the whiteboards out the windows, blowing up the school, throwing all the books in a heap and setting fire to them. The kind of thing you say when it's lovely and warm outside, for example, and you just couldn't be bothered doing school work. But nobody had ever *actually* gathered all the books into a heap and set them alight. If someone did do such a crazy thing, it would be someone whose head was seriously messed up, and everyone would try to stop him.

Same goes for the Flemish Giant idea. Sure, Fridz is

dead cross with this Kristine, because she's taken her dad away – that much Konrad gets – and because she is so cross, she wishes a plague on Kristine. And there's no doubt about it, it would be kind of fun to get up Kristine's nose with this mega-rabbit belonging to Fridz's dad. But no sane person would *really* play such a mean trick, Konrad thinks.

Like many other people, Konrad thinks he knows what a sane person looks like, and how he or she behaves. A sane person, he thinks, looks much like Konrad Bantelmann of The Dransfeld and a sane person would never do anything that Konrad Bantelmann would not do. So far, so good.

But – there is, unfortunately, a but. The thing is that even though he really likes Fridz, Konrad has certain doubts about whether she's a sane person. That is to say, a sane person on the Konrad Bantelmann model. There is something about her that suggests she is not only nice and likeable, but also a teeny bit mad. Maybe even mad enough to try to put this rabbit plan into action. And maybe so mad that even a person as thoroughly sane as Konrad Bantelmann might be persuaded to go along with her.

Thinking these thoughts, it takes no time at all to get to number 28b, even though Konrad has been walking fairly slowly. And now here he is at the door.

Konrad realises that on his way here, he has split into two Konrads. Two very different Konrads. One of the Konrads is really scared of getting mixed up in this rabbit thing. That's the old Konrad. The other Konrad, however, is getting butterflies in his tummy at the thought that he could really take part in such a great adventure! This is a new Konrad.

Together, these two Konrads press the doorbell. Less than three seconds later, the door is swung open. And as usual, Fridz grabs the double Konrad by the arm and yanks him into the house.

'At last!' she cries. 'Where on earth have you been? Did you fall asleep on your feet?'

But she doesn't wait for him to answer.

'Come on!' she cries. 'You'll be amazed. Everything's ready'

Watching her scuttle down the stairs to the cellar, the two Konrads are convinced that since yesterday she has not thought about a single thing except the giant rabbit revenge plan.

Oh dear, thinks the old Konrad. *Well, let's just wait and see,* the other one, the new one, says soothingly.

Down in the cellar, Fridz takes a key out of her pocket and unlocks one of the cellar rooms. In the Bantelmanns' house that would be the cellar where they keep provisions. But God only knows what you might expect to find here in number 28b.

Fridz opens the door and stands aside.

'So,' she says, 'what do you think?'

The Konrads say nothing. In the cellar, the one that is supposed to contain provisions – where, in the Bantelmanns' house there are lots of bottles and tins, all clean and tidy and arranged on handy shelves in order of size – there is nothing of the kind. No. Here there are only more packing cases. Big ones and little ones, a few actually folded up, but most of them just thrown here and there.

'Well?' says Fridz. She seems to be delighted by these boxes.

'Boxes,' say the Konrads. Nothing to be all that very thrilled about.

'Yes, exactly,' says Fridz. 'Any number of super boxes. So we can send the stupid cow her rabbit plague. Without her knowing who has sent it.'

The old Konrad is not very surprised. He knew all along. But the new Konrad had wanted to wait and see what would happen. The old one just has to try and make the best of it now.

'So are you really going to do it?' he says.

Fridz has already started to push some of the packing cases aside.

'What are you saying?' she says. 'It was your idea in the first place.'

Oh good lord! The old Konrad remembers: he did say something yesterday about setting a trap, but this idea with the rabbit – Fridz had thought that up all by herself. And in any case, he'd only meant to say something funny to cheer her up.

He was just about to say this in his defence, but the way Fridz is all business with these boxes, it doesn't look as if she would be interested in getting involved in a complicated conversation about who said what and who didn't.

She is tossing them around at such a rate that the boxes are practically whizzing by the Konrads' ears. And now at last she lifts one up with both hands over her head and cries, 'This is the one! I'd hidden it under the others, just to be on the safe side.'

You'd need to do that all right with this one, because it looks totally different from all the others. It's bright red, which is to say, it has been covered with bright red paper. And on top of that, several metres of luminous yellow ribbon has been wrapped around it, and on top of the box is the fattest, most crooked bow that the Konrads have ever seen.

'Wow!' they both say.

'Exactly!' says Fridz. She is looking very proud and that makes her look pretty. She turns the box around so that it can be seen from all sides.

'It took me two hours yesterday to make it look like this. Good, isn't it?'

Right. Even if you wanted to contradict her, you couldn't do it.

What a box! On the top is an address label, written in three different colours and decorated all over with little hearts.

'What do you think?' says Fridz, making big eyes. 'Just imagine how that cow will fall on it! She'll think the biggest, fattest present in the world is in it. And then –' She presses the box to her chest, and dances around in a circle like an Indian. 'Then she'll tear the paper off and with her long fingernails she'll pull the lid off, and she'll reach in with her two greedy hands – and what will she pull out?'

But before the Konrads can say anything, Fridz lets the box fall and pretends she has something in her hands. She gives this something a crazed look and starts screeching, 'Eeeeeeek! Eeeeeeek! A rabbit! Help! Help!'

Then she pretends to chuck the thing away from her, and immediately she starts scratching herself all over. 'Eeeeeeek!' she keeps shouting. 'I'm coming out in a rash! My hair is falling out! I'm blue all over, and green! My teeth are going black! My toenails are curling up! Help! Help!'

Finally, she puts her hands around her throat and presses hard. 'I can't breathe!' she gasps hoarsely, rolling her eyes. 'I have a multinational animal fur allergy and I must, unfortunately, die a bit.'

She takes one hand from her throat and waves it at the Konrads. 'Goodbye, cruel world!' she rasps. 'Do me a favour. Tell the graveyard rabbits not to dig in my grave.' Then she lets herself drop, stiff as an iron bar, in among the boxes.

But she's back on her feet again within seconds.

'What did you think of that?' she says.

But she doesn't get an answer. The two Konrads have fallen on the floor with laughter. And they are still lying there, tears running down their cheeks, gasping for breath.

'Hey,' says Fridz, 'what's all this hanging about? We have work to do. The rabbit has to go in the box.'

The old Konrad, the sensible one, gets his breath back first.

'What?' he says. He expects the worst – and he expects right.

'You have to help me,' says Fridz.

'I can't!'

Oops! Who said that? Sentences like 'I can't' are strictly forbidden, especially in front of girls.

Punishment comes, as deserved.

'Don't get your knickers in a twist,' says Fridz. 'Here, look!'

She takes the box, its bow now a bit more crooked, and presses it into the Konrads' hands. The box has a flap on the side, which looks as if it has been cut with a pair of shears. Fridz opens the flap and closes it.

'See?' she says. 'You hold the flap of the box open. Giant in. Flap closed. You can manage that much. Let's go. We haven't got much time. Henri will be back in half an hour.'

What can he do? Nothing, of course. To be on the safe side, the old Konrad gives the new one, the adventurous one, the bright red box – and two minutes later there he is, in front of the hutch, helping Fridz to take her revenge on her father's girlfriend.

'Keep still, would you!' says Fridz. She does not, however, mean the Konrads, even though their hands are pretty shaky. She means the rabbit, who apparently has got wind of what's going on, and who is therefore not going to let himself be caught.

'I am keeping still,' says the new Konrad, because he can't see anything from behind the box.

'I don't mean you,' says Fridz.

And now she has nabbed the last Flemish Giant.

'Flap open!' she cries.

The new Konrad holds the flap open as wide as it goes. His eyes, however, he keeps shut. And when he notices how heavy the box suddenly gets, and how at the same time it starts to rumble inside, he panics a bit.

'Close flap!' calls Fridz.

But the new Konrad can't do it. The best he can manage is not to let this ton weight of a creaking box fall.

Fridz says something unrepeatable and closes the flap herself. She takes a big roll of sticky tape out of her pocket and a huge pair of scissors, and she uses a couple of pieces of sticky tape to stick the flap together so tightly that a dozen rabbits couldn't get it open. At least, that's what she says as she finishes doing the sticking.

'You can put it down now.'

Which the new but no longer quite so adventurous Konrad is delighted to do.

'But only for a quick breather,' says Fridz. 'We have to go immediately.'

'Where are we going?'

'Well, where do you think? To the post office, of course.'

Now even the new Konrad protests vigorously. 'Not to the post office!' he cries.

'Why not?'

Why not? Why not! How could he even begin to explain? Heavens above! Send a rabbit in a box by post! First of all, there is no way the post people will allow it. And secondly they would be perfectly right, because it would be pure cruelty to animals.

'What do you mean, cruelty to animals?' says Fridz, kicking the box. 'He's got space in there. And if you think it's necessary, I can make a few air holes.' She's already holding the giant scissors over the box.

'It's no use!' Konrad is all worked up. 'For goodness

sake!' he says. 'Parcels get thrown all over the place! The rabbit's bones will get broken!'

Fridz says nothing for a few seconds. That is unusual for her. She must be thinking. And if she's thinking, then probably she'll say something. But what?

'So,' she says at last, 'why does it sometimes say *Fragile* on parcels? What do you think? Obviously because breakable things are being transported. Even things made of glass. And if glass can be transported in boxes, then there's no fear of the Belgian here.'

She kicks the box again. Then she disappears and the two Konrads look at each other.

'See!' says the old one. 'There you go.'

'Hmm,' says the new one.

For a moment, it looks as if they are going to have a row. But then they both decide to work together. Because for the next bit, you need to have your wits about you.

Five minutes later, Fridz is back in the garage. She has painted an enormous label saying *Fragile* but it hasn't got any little hearts on it. She sticks the label on the box with sticky tape.

Konrad tries again. 'But it's so far to the post office,' he says. 'All the way to the supermarket. We'll never make it.'

'Of course we will,' says Fridz. 'Just you wait and see.'

She signals to Konrad and the two of them carry the box out of the garage into the garden.

'So,' says Fridz. 'You're whacked already, are you?'

Konrad looks around him. This is not a garden anyway. On either side there are gardens, with shrubs and little trees, just like in the Bantelmann garden and in the gardens of the neighbours of number 17a. And just like there, the new lawns are starting to grow. The new lawn, on which for ages and ages no one was allowed to walk. But here in the middle, where the garden of number 28b ought to be, there is nothing but a hilly lunar landscape of thick black earth. Here and there are plants that Mum Bantelmann would certainly call weeds, and further back you can see quite clearly the caterpillar tracks of a bulldozer or a digger. Atrocious!

Or maybe not. Konrad imagines what a good place this would be for playing Landing on an Unknown Planet. Or Digging for Treasure on a Desert Island.

'Don't gape like that!' says Fridz. 'The people next door do enough of that.'

But it's a nice garden.

'If Henri doesn't manage to get a gardener soon,' she says, 'they'll send us one of those notices about prohibited seed dispersal.'

'Because . . . ?'

'Because our weeds will start growing next door too. Man!' says Fridz. 'Forget the stupid garden. Look here!'

Oh, right. On the patio there's a wooden trolley just big enough to fit the Flemish Giant box on. And that's what is going to happen.

There's no going back now, thinks Konrad.

Fridz gives a signal, and together they lift the box onto the trolley.

'Now we need to go out on the road,' says Fridz. 'You pull. And I'll watch out.'

Konrad pulls. The wheels of the little wooden trolley squeak horribly. But he hardly hears it. What is he like! he's thinking. A fairly large boy pulling a squeaking trolley with a big red box on it. Not to mention the big yellow bow.

Now they're on the road. Did the flowery net curtains of number 27b move? Lena and Lisa! Or Lara and Lana? Not that it matters. Konrad has the extremely unpleasant sensation that he is making a total fool of himself.

'Watch where you're going!' says Fridz. 'Head up! Veer right a bit. And get a move on!'

When they arrive at a point where they could be seen from number 17a, Konrad wishes he could disappear into thin air, but luckily no one is looking. In fact, the whole Dransfeld is like a morgue.

After a fairly strenuous half hour, they finally arrive at the supermarket by the junction.

Return to Sender

There is a yellow notice above the entrance to the supermarket indicating that there's a sub-post office here.

That's handy, thinks Konrad. That's not his own opinion though. It's just that the sentence 'That's handy' is regularly uttered by all the Bantelmanns' neighbours in The Dransfeld when mention is made of the sub-post office in the supermarket. Probably specially for the new Dransfelders. So that they don't have to travel all the way into town to the main post office with their letters and parcels, but instead can do their postal business, very handily, in the supermarket before or after shopping.

But now it's not so handy. On the contrary; it's almost a catastrophe. Because it suddenly dawns on Konrad why The Dransfeld was so quiet this morning that they were able to get out of there completely unnoticed and unchallenged with the squeaky trolley and the ridiculous red Flemish Giant box. It's because the Dransfelders are all shopping.

And there will certainly be someone here whom Konrad Bantelmann from number 17a visited last week in order to complete his list of children. Even one would be enough to destroy him. Because of course the post office will refuse to transport a rabbit, and there will be a huge to-do and to make matters worse, all the Dransfelders will get to hear about the unspeakable revenge story. Konrad Bantelmann is dispatching allergy-rabbits, they'll all be saying. And what's more, he dispatches them with girls. And then Konrad Bantelmann can go back to using his Dransfeld notebook as an exercise book again. Or at best as a complete list of the Dransfeld children with whom he will never play again, not for a single minute, because they will think him completely mad. They'll end by calling him Bunny Konni. The thought of it!

'What's wrong?' says Fridz. 'Legs turned to lead?'

If only that was all! Konrad wishes for a miracle. Please, please, he thinks. And then once more: please. Maybe the automatic doors of the supermarket will have some secret mechanism that makes them refuse to open when someone tries to smuggle in a giant rabbit in a box. For my sake, thinks Konrad.

Animals, after all, are not allowed in the supermarket. And rules like this have to be obeyed. Konrad Bantelmann has always had a fairly relaxed, one might even say friendly, relationship with rules. He doesn't like them much, no one does. But breaking them he likes even less. Never before has Konrad Bantelmann so desperately wished that a rule would be enforced.

'Go on,' says Fridz.

Whoosh goes the automatic door, and of course it opens. A special miracle just for Konrad Bantelmann was never really on the cards.

Inside the supermarket nothing happens at first. The people go on shopping and the shop assistant at the vegetable counter goes on arranging tomatoes in boxes. Nobody looks twice at the monster of a red box with the crooked yellow bow.

People are completely insensitive, thinks Konrad. Otherwise, he doesn't think about very much. He even tries to give up thinking altogether. He'd be quite happy to give up breathing and seeing too. But that wouldn't do. He has to be able to see where he is pulling the trolley so that he doesn't bang into the shelves. And you do have to breathe.

There is music playing in the supermarket. It helps people to shop, Dad said once. Music soothes you, and then you're not afraid any more that you might spend too much money. Konrad wishes now that the music would soothe him. But the opposite is the case. This music makes him feel as if he is in one of those TV police dramas that he is not allowed to watch. They always have music, especially when things are getting really dangerous.

'This way,' says Fridz.

They get through the automatic barrier with some difficulty, then it's on past the vegetable counter and the fruit stand. Just around the corner is the yellow post-office counter with a couple of yellow shelves behind it and a big weighing-scales beside it. They go up to it, and plonk the bright red box on the scales. The pointer bends way over to the left.

'Well, well,' says someone. 'I wonder who's going to get such a heavy present.'

This someone is the man behind the post office counter. Konrad knows this, even though he is not looking up, but is instead looking with great interest at the floor.

'It's written on it,' says Fridz.

Great, thinks Konrad. This girl has put him in one of the most embarrassing positions that he has ever been in in his whole life. All the same, he has to admire her. What a smart answer! 'It's written on it.' Just like that. Konrad couldn't even answer if someone asked him his name, or how much two and two is.

'Well, let's see then,' says the voice of the post office. 'What a wonderful box! Wouldn't I love to know what's in it!'

The voice is loud. And when he looks up briefly, Konrad sees that two women are breaking off from their work to take a look at the box.

'I'd bet . . . I'd bet . . . gold bars!' says the loud voice of the post office.

Gold – gold, of all things! A word that everyone finds interesting. Including the people in the supermarket. At least a dozen of them are now crowding round the post office counter and staring. Konrad pretends he needs to tie his shoelace.

'Or maybe,' says the voice of the post office, 'precious stones and diamonds.'

Konrad can see nothing but legs as he goes on tying his shoelace. Female legs, male legs, even a few children's legs. He goes on doggedly tying his shoelace.

Above him, pens are being scratched on paper, something is being torn, and there's a hollow knocking sound. 'Eighteen euro eighty,' says the voice of the post office and then money jingles on the counter. Could it be that the whole thing is going to go off all right? Konrad, the eternal lace-tier, hardly dares to hope. He gets up very slowly.

Then something goes 'Wump!' And again: 'Wumpety-bump!'

At the same time, the bright red box bounces a bit to the right on the scales, making the pointer sway frantically from right to left.

'Well, well, well!' says the man to whom the voice of the post office belongs. 'What the hell is in here?'

Fate, take your course, thinks Konrad. That's what Mum always says when she pours drinking chocolate for Peter and everyone is quite sure that it will get knocked over today as usual.

'Something fragile,' says Fridz. 'That's written on it too.' She taps her finger on the *Fragile* label.

Brave, thinks Konrad. But probably useless.

How right he is!

'Tell me,' the post-office man starts carefully, but also rather sternly, 'is the fragile something in this box also a living something?'

Is Fridz going to deny that a Flemish Giant is a living thing? He wouldn't put it past her. But no, she doesn't.

'It's a rabbit,' she says loudly. 'But never fear, Mr Post Director, it'll keep quiet.'

'I *see*,' says the postman. 'However, it isn't really a question of whether or not your rabbit will stay quiet. We at the post office are not allowed to transport living animals in boxes. It's not good for the animals, and it's not good for the post office either. The animals might die of thirst. Or they might smother. Or they might escape and damage the sorting machines.'

'Oh, really?' says Fridz pretty snippily. 'You learn something new every day.'

'You certainly do,' says the post-office man. He gives her back the money and makes a fat slash with a felt pen across the address label on the box.

Konrad has also learnt something new. Something very important, in fact. He has learnt that being right and being proved right are not necessarily all that fantastic. Because he has been proved right: the post office certainly does not dispatch live rabbits. But what good is that to him?

For after Fridz has taken back her money, she looks at him as if it was all his fault. He, the sane Konrad, and not her, the mad Friederike, or the post office man or the very sane post office. She doesn't say, 'Oh dear, I should have listened to my new friend, to the sane Konrad Bantelmann.' Oh, no. She glowers at him, as if he had brought her, on purpose and out of sheer spite, to such a pretty pass with the post office.

'Well, get hold of it,' she says venomously. And after they have put the box back on the trolley, she biffs him one so hard that he almost falls over.

If only that was all! A venomous Friederike Konrad might be able to put up with. But as they pull the trolley out of the supermarket, people are crowding around on all sides, customers with their shopping bags, staff in their white shop coats. The supermarket music is playing a particularly cheerful piece, and they are all gawking, their eyes out on sticks. All Konrad needs now is for them to clap. Applause for the two daftest children in the whole Dransfeld.

Konrad looks intently at the ground again, even though he knows it doesn't help. So, it's happened, he thinks. Sure as eggs is eggs, someone will have recognised him. In the space of a quarter of an hour he will be the laughing stock of The Dransfeld. No one will ever play with him again. Not even if his dad owned seven toy shops.

Whoosh, goes the automatic door again, luckily, and the two of them are out in the supermarket car park with their squeaky trolley.

Fridz utters a single word – such a dreadful word that Konrad decides immediately to take absolutely no notice of it.

'I told you so,' he says. Which does not make things better.

'Yeah, yeah,' says Fridz. And then she repeats the dreadful word.

Too bad, thinks Konrad. He can't let it go. 'They don't carry living animals.'

'Oh, stop gloating, Mr Know-it-all.' Fridz kicks the trolley. 'Pull, would you! I want to go home.'

And so the two of them make their way back to The Dransfeld. It's much the same as it was on the way to the post office. The bright red box with the crooked bow sits on the trolley, the trolley squeaks, Konrad pulls and Fridz goes alongside and watches out. And once again, nothing is said.

But there are also differences. On the way, nothing was

said because Konrad was not feeling comfortable. Nothing is said this time, because Friederike Frenke is cross. And because Konrad Bantelmann is offended; so offended that when they get to number 17a, he hands the trolley over to Fridz, says goodbye, rings the doorbell and runs up the steps past his astonished mother. Whereupon Fridz calls out 'Pffff!' and then she says something else very quietly and goes on alone.

In his room, Konrad gets his mouse Mattchoo from under the duvet and tells him for a whole quarter of an hour what sort of a terrible person this Fridz is. And in the end, he even tells him what a dreadful word she said.

Mattchoo muggers his disgust.

The Double Forest Snake

What a day! Konrad spends the rest of the morning and the whole afternoon being offended. It's not much fun, but he can't do anything else. Shortly before supper, his mood improves a little.

But then, unfortunately, there's a performance with the drinking chocolate. Peter not only knocks over his mug, but this time, for a change, it falls from a height of about twenty centimetres onto the china plate that holds the cheese and the cold meats, and the gouda and the slices of parma ham are completely soaked. Konrad tries to save the day. Too bad! Because although he does succeed in fishing Peter's cup out of the sea of chocolate, it slips out of his fingers and cracks against the china plate, and the chocolate overflows and quickly spreads itself all over the whole table.

It's the same as usual, only worse. Dad rants, Mum runs into the kitchen, both of them shouting 'Don't touch anything!' and 'Stay where you are!' as well as other, considerably uglier things about children who are incapable of drinking their chocolate without flooding whole half-duplexes.

In the end, Konrad counts how many absorbent kitchen towels are used to mop up the contents of a mug of chocolate. Twenty-three. That could be a record. Peter cries all the time, exceptionally loudly. He is still of an age to think that unusually loud crying is a protection against being scolded. That is, however, a misapprehension. It's just that if you cry loud enough, you don't hear the scolding. It would be much better just to pull a face and to look at the ground with a concerned expression. Dad has demonstrated this a couple of times and Konrad can do it, but unfortunately Peter can't do it yet. His nerves are bad, he said once.

When the chocolate is finally mopped up, they try to dry off the gouda and the slices of parma ham, using yet more kitchen towels. It goes quite well at first, but then lots of little fluffy bits from the paper towels begin to stick to the cheese and the ham and in the effort to scrub the fluffy bits off, the cheese and the ham are so badly damaged that you can't really tell them apart any more. Whereupon Mum finally says that there will be three days of cheese and ham bake, because that way it doesn't really matter much if you can't distinguish the cheese from the ham. And it doesn't matter either if there are still a few bits of paper towel fluff sticking to the food.

That's rough, and not just because of the fluffy bits. Konrad is no fan of cheese and ham bake. It tastes basically quite good, but you can't tell what it is that you're eating. When Konrad prises the cheesy top off, he gets a faceful of steam, and he also gets the idea that Mum could easily have smuggled other things, apart from potatoes, ham and cheese, into the bake – stuff he would not eat if he could see what it was. Mum is quite capable of doing this kind of thing.

But it gets worse because when the table is dry again, Dad says that as a punishment for this record-breaking messing, he's not going to tell the next instalment of the story of the forest snake and the mysterious crystal.

Ka-boom! Not tell any more of the story? This is really harsh. No story is the most extreme punishment that there is in the Bantelmann house. It only exists for the most unimaginably appalling crimes against the rules of human co-existence, Dad says.

There is one remaining hope, however. Because always in the Bantelmann house, when punishments are handed down, Konrad and Peter are allowed to bring forward so-called mitigating circumstances. These are reasons which so reduce the guilt of the guilty that the punishment is either lessened or indeed completely revoked.

Mitigating circumstances in the matter of knocking over chocolate are many and varied. And they are also tried and tested. Some of them have proved themselves to be good, and some to be bad. This one, for example, is rather bad: 'The cup was so slippery' or 'It was so sticky.' It's amazing, really, because the cup often is either slippery or sticky, because someone has put their wet or honey-smeared fingers all over it. But the Bantelmann parents seem to think that one is responsible for the slipperiness or stickiness of one's own fingers, and therefore they do not allow this as a mitigating circumstance.

This, on the other hand, is a very good mitigating circumstance: 'I am so tired.' This only works, of course, in the evening. And it is very important to yawn all over the spilt chocolate, not to eat any more and to really want to go to bed. If all these factors coalesce, then 'I am so tired' is in most cases accepted as a mitigating circumstance. Sometimes the parents don't even scold the chocolate-knocker-over any more, but simply reproach each other for not making sure that their children get enough sleep.

But today it does not look as if one of the old mitigating circumstances will do. The mess was far too record-breaking for that. All the same, Konrad gives it a go. Because firstly, something has to be done about reducing this punishment; secondly, Peter is crying much more loudly and more shrilly than usual; thirdly – well, thirdly, there is something that Konrad really wants to find out today. What it is, he's not entirely sure, but he knows that his best chance of finding it out is if the story of the forest snake is told. And so he produces his mitigating circumstance, one he himself considers the most absurd of all those they have ever tried, but nothing else occurs to him. He says, 'We couldn't help it because . . . because . . . '

'Because?' says Dad, as Mum takes the cheese carefully into the kitchen.

'Because we are still so new here.' So there, it's out, the most ridiculous excuse.

'New?' says Dad. 'Here? Where here? At the dining table? In the world?'

'In The Dransfeld,' says Konrad.

'Oho!' goes Dad, as if he understands. 'I see. And in The Dransfeld mugs weigh much more than elsewhere. Of course. They have a different specific weight here. How could I have forgotten?'

Of course, Dad doesn't see at all. He is just being ironic.

Being ironic means pretending to accept a ridiculous reason for knocking over chocolate in order to be able later to hand down the worst punishment after all. Then come noises from the kitchen. First comes 'Clink!' And then 'Crash!'

'Huh!' says Mum.

Dad and Konrad run into the kitchen. Not Peter. He has to go on roaring.

Mum has let a plate fall. 'It's true,' she says. 'The plate was definitely heavier than usual. I couldn't hold it, and it just fell.' She looks at Dad.

'Unheard of,' says Dad. 'We'll have to get a team of scientists to come and investigate this phenomenon. Clearly, my sons are totally innocent.'

At which point Peter stops crying as suddenly as if someone had pulled out a plug.

'By the way,' says Dad. 'My first-born son was with his girlfriend again today. So, how did it go? Did you enjoy yourself?'

'Konrad,' says Mum quickly. 'Will you please get a new kitchen roll out of the cellar.'

Konrad goes. He goes very quickly and very gladly. But before he is out the door, he sees Mum making frantic signs at Dad.

Two hours later, Konrad and Peter are lying again on either side of Dad in Peter's bed, trying to kick him as little as possible in the stomach.

'So, I'll continue,' begins Dad, 'at the point where Franzkarl Findouter and his expedition team are considering the problem of how they can get the mysterious crystal out of its hiding place in the middle of nowhere and into a research laboratory, so that its mysterious powers can be investigated. Because that's the only place they can do the experiments that will lead to their being awarded the Nobble Prize.'

'Yes!' says Peter. It all sounds so delightful that he kicks Dad a bit in the stomach.

'But this plan,' says Dad, 'is a call to action to Anabasis the forest snake. Because its one task is to guard the crystal against being captured by aliens.'

'But unfortunately,' says Konrad, 'it can't do a thing about it.'

'Excuse me?' say Dad and Peter.

'It can't do a thing.'

'And why not?' Why not! Who's telling this story anyway?

'I don't know,' says Konrad. 'But anyway, it can think of nothing. Maybe it is wounded somehow.'

'Or cross,' suggests Peter.

'Aha,' says Dad. 'Right. Possibly something very peculiar and unsettling has happened that could have a not insignificant influence on the rest of our story. Hmm. What do you think it is?'

Of course, neither of them has a clue.

'Well,' says Dad, 'possibly something has happened that until now nobody has ever observed and of which there is not a single mention in all the scientific books.'

Dad pauses. For a moment, Konrad fears that not even Dad knows what this remarkable incident might be. But he's wrong there.

'Imagine,' says Dad, 'that in the night, Anabasis the forest snake has split in two. What do you think of that?'

What could they say? Split? The forest snake? And into what, if you please?

'Into Ana the forest snake and Basis the forest snake.'

'Oh,' says Peter.

'Hmm,' goes Konrad.

'Granted,' says Dad, 'this is definitely a bit dodgy. So anyway, it turns out that Anabasis the forest snake has in fact, for unimaginable aeons, consisted of two snakes, which, astonishingly, are both capable of hanging on by their teeth to the other one's tail in such a way that there is a completely harmonious relationship between them. So that we are no longer looking at two but at a single forest snake. Effectively, a couple-snake.'

'Or a cobble-snake,' says Peter.

'Or a cobble-snake,' says Dad, although he doesn't find the word entirely suitable.

'There's no such thing, is there?' says Konrad.

'Of course there is!' Dad explains it again. 'And don't forget,' he says, 'that when they are coupled together, then Ana and Basis don't even know themselves that they are not one but two snakes.'

'Hmm,' says Konrad. 'And why would that be?'

'Well,' says Dad. 'It's a highly intelligent way to conserve energy. One thinks for two and two work as one.' Dad is dead proud of this explanation.

'Hmm,' says Konrad again. 'And which one is in front?'

'It varies.'

'But surely Ana must always be in front?'

'Why?'

'Because otherwise it would be Basisana.'

'Basisana!' cries Peter. He likes this name.

'Well,' says Dad. 'I'll have to think about that one.' But he'd rather not do that for the moment. 'What's happening right now,' he says, 'is this: the forest snake has split in two in the night, but apparently the two individual snakes have not, as is usually the case, re-coupled after a bit of a chat. Instead, they have remained separate. You follow?'

'Sure,' says Konrad. He has worked out that further technical questions would probably hamper the continuation of the story.

'Well, then, let's go on,' says Dad. 'Because the most important thing is coming up. The moment they separate, the two forest snakes start to quarrel about what they should do to prevent the abduction of the crystal.'

'A quarrel?' says Konrad. Now, this is interesting.

'Absolutely,' says Dad, 'and a pretty bad quarrel it is. Quarrels are always bad, but when two people are squabbling who otherwise never squabble and live in perfect harmony, then of course it is much worse.'

'True!' says Konrad. 'But why?'

'Well, in the first place, they are disappointed that they, of all people, are arguing, because they had thought that such a thing could never happen. And secondly . . . well, secondly, when people who like each other fight, then it hurts a lot.'

'Ah,' says Konrad. 'And why is that?'

'Because they have no code of conflict.'

'Code of conflict?'

'Rules of warfare.'

As if there could be such a thing! Rules about fighting.

'Oh yes,' says Dad. 'For example, if you have a code of conflict, then you don't just run off and sulk after a fight. Instead, you sit down quietly and you think what you could do to settle the argument.'

'Even if you are very angry?'

'Even then,' says Dad.

'Even if the fight was absolutely not your fault?'

'Aha!' says Dad. 'Here we have an excellent example of how a code of conflict works. If you have a code of conflict, then you know that there is never only one person who is to blame for the fight. And if you know that, then you can see past your own nose and – how shall I put it –,' Dad thinks, and then he laughs and says, 'and offer the hand of friendship and reconciliation. Or something like that.'

For a few seconds, nobody says anything.

Then Peter says something. He says, 'Forest snake!' But what he means is, Are you ever going to tell us any more of this story?

'Okay,' says Dad. And then, even though it is nearly a quarter past eight, he tells in great detail about how the two forest snakes Ana and Basis fought about the best way of protecting the crystal against abduction.

It was a bad quarrel. The rather contrary Ana wants to bite all the members of the expedition before dawn with her left poison fang, which contains a sleeping potion that puts people to sleep for two whole days.

'Oh dear,' says Konrad.

The more peaceable Basis doesn't see the point of this. He'd rather just do nothing. After all, they have no idea why they are supposed to be guarding this crystal, so why not take this opportunity to find out at last what the whole business is about? Why not let the explorers explore away, and they could keep watch and only intervene when the state of scientific knowledge is showing a marked improvement?

'Well . . .' says Konrad.

But this sounds far too sensible for the tempestuous Ana. Their task is to guard the crystal, and that's that. And because this whole thing has made her even more tempestuous than usual, now she suggests biting the explorers with her *right* fang, which contains something much worse – tickle poison.

'What's tickle poison?' asks Peter.

'Hah!' cries Dad. 'You've never heard of the dreaded tickle poison? This is how it works!' And with that he leaps on Konrad and tickles him so hard that Konrad gets completely red in the face and can't breathe for laughing.

'Me too!' says Peter. 'Please!'

Peter can't bear being tickled. He starts to roar if anyone so much as threatens to tickle him, but – ah, sweet mystery of life! – if there is one thing he can bear even less than being tickled it's his older brother being tickled when he is not.

'Fair enough,' says Dad and then he jumps on Peter. Three seconds later, Peter is begging him to stop, but in the general mêlée, nobody can understand what he is saying, and so Dad goes on tickling him for a bit.

'You see,' he says at last. 'That's how the dangerous tickle poison works. An overdose of it can kill.'

Konrad is the first to be able to speak again. 'So, what happens about the fight between Ana and Basis?'

'A bad scene,' says Dad. 'The two of them haven't the smallest notion of the code of conflict. On the contrary. The more they fight, the stupider and the more locked-in they get. Ana wants to bite everything to bits, regardless of how much venom she uses up. And Basis says that basically he doesn't want to guard the wretched old sparkler any more and if these explorers want to have it, they can stick it up their jumpers and jolly well jump in the lake with it for all he cares.

'And so on and so forth. At the end of the day, one says yes just because the other says no. And the other says no just because the first one says yes.'

'And then?' says Konrad.

'Well,' says Dad. 'Then something happens that sometimes does happen. Suddenly, the two forest snakes become so ashamed of all this fighting that, right at the same moment, they both decide to make up. And how do you think they do this?'

'Dunno.'

'Easy! They link up together again. But because they both decide to do it at the same time, they each grab the other by the tail. Ana bites into Basis's tail and Basis bites into Ana's.'

'Hoi,' says Konrad.

'And so,' says Dad, 'there they lie, like a discarded bicycle tyre. Completely reconciled but thick as a brick. Ana thinks Basis is in front and turns off her thinking. And Basis thinks Ana is in front, and also turns off his thinking.'

'So now they'll never be able to split up again!'

'The poor things,' says Peter, sounding as if he might cry.

'Oh well.' Dad sighs as he gets up out of Peter's bed. 'They can think just a tiny little bit. Enough, in any case, to let go again after a few minutes, at the same time. And then –,' Dad is out of the bed now, 'then the pair of them make off in two different directions and disappear into the impenetrable jungle.'

He kisses the two boys on the forehead. 'Just like you two now' he says. 'And no fighting, right?'

'Right,' they say together.

Fridz's Next Plan

The next day, Thursday, about two hours after breakfast, Konrad Bantelmann is pressing the index finger of his right hand on the doorbell of number 28b, Hedwig Dransfeld Strasse. His left hand is in his pocket, clutching the new code of conflict.

The new code of conflict consists of precisely eight sentences, which he wrote this morning, in the two hours after breakfast, on a clean page in his Dransfeld nobebook.

He can hear the bell ringing inside the house, and soon the door swings open.

'You?' says Fridz. 'I wasn't expecting you of all people.'

'Yeah, well,' says Konrad, 'I'm not all people, am I?' What a stupid thing to say! What he'd actually meant to say was the first sentence of the new code of conflict. But somehow it just didn't come out right. Oh dear, thinks Konrad. Not a good start.

But it's a good start after all, because Fridz laughs at his pathetic attempt at a joke. Then she asks, 'Are you in better form?' and without waiting for an answer, she drags him into the house, banging the door.

As if it mattered what kind of form he was in, considering what lousy form she'd been in yesterday! Konrad would like to say this, but it wouldn't be in keeping with the new code of conflict. Instead, he says what he had resolved to say: the first sentence on the piece of paper that was in his pocket.

'Hello, Fridz,' he says. 'I came today to say to you –'

But he doesn't get any further.

'What's wrong with you? You sound as if you are about to recite a birthday poem or something. It's too late. My birthday was on the ninth of May.'

Keep calm, Konrad Bantelmann. Quite calm! 'I came today to say to you –'

'That we have to do things differently,' says Fridz.

'That's exactly what I was thinking!'

She rolls her eyes. 'Of course we have to do it differently. You just can't send a rabbit by post. Every schoolchild knows that. A live animal in a box? How silly! Only a dumb cluck could come up with something like that. No, no. That won't do.'

This is totally mad! Konrad squeezes his eyes closed. He feels like a firework whose string someone has lit and which is about to burst into flames in a gunpowder store. He is just about to fly straight up in the air, explode on the landing of number 28b and come twinkling back down in the form of a million sparks. What sort of nonsense is this Fridz talking now? But before he explodes and goes up in the air, himself and his lovely code of conflict, Konrad sees Fridz once more through the narrow slits of his eyes, and she is grinning. A nice, big, wide grin.

Would Friederike Frenke ever have a code of conflict? If so, Konrad thinks, it would probably look quite different from his.

He closes his fist carefully over his eight sentences. 'Right,' he says. 'What happened yesterday was stupid.'

'Exactly what I say,' says Fridz.

And then she gives Konrad a kiss. For the second time. Very quickly, and luckily just on the cheek again. But still, a kiss is a kiss.

Konrad blushes. Only three days ago he had been in a state because he had a date with a girl, and now he's constantly being kissed by her. A dreadful state of affairs.

'Let's go!' says Fridz, pointing towards the basement. 'We have loads to do. Let's get started!'

Hold on a minute! What's all this? After the disaster they had yesterday, surely she's given up that terrible plan of hers. To hell with this let's-send-an-allergy-rabbit-to-Kristine-Crisis project. Right?

'Will we play a bit of *Crazy Bugs*?' says Konrad. Well, you have to try.

'What? Oh, come on!'

'Is your mum here?' This is Konrad's last hope. Mabye the whole crazy business won't happen if Fridz's mum is there. Parents have this amazing ability to call a halt to, or at least to lessen, all the monkey business that's going on around them, just by being there. On the other hand, Fridz's mum is not exactly a byword for common sense and Konrad-Bantelmannish behaviour. Konrad has worked this much out by now.

'So what if she is?' says Fridz. 'Anyway, she has to go to the bank.'

A door opens upstairs and Fridz's mum comes down into the hall.

Fridz digs Konrad in the ribs. 'All your fault,' she says softly. 'We could have been down in the basement by now.'

Fridz's mum has tied her hair up in a knot. She's very pale again. She looks as if she has been crying.

'Have you seen my folder?' she asks.

'Which folder?'

'The red one. No, the blue one.' Fridz's mum sits on the bottom step of the stairs. 'Oh, hello, Konrad! Are you planning to play something nice today?'

'Ah,' says Konrad.

'I mean, like yesterday, the way you played Christmas in the middle of summer! The people across the road told me about it. And you were Rudolf the Red-Nosed Reindeer, the one that pulls the sleigh.'

Rudolf the Red-Nosed Reindeer! Oh, ground, open up! Konrad even taps on it with his foot. But alas, the ground has no intention of opening up. For the moment.

'It was his idea,' says Fridz.

'Sweet,' says Fridz's mum. 'But if I don't find this folder, we may as well move out.'

'Maybe it's in the oven,' says Fridz. 'Or in the fridge. There's loads of room in there.'

'Cheeky monkey!' says her mum.

Then she hits herself on the forehead. 'In the car! That's where it is, for sure.' She looks at the clock. 'It's high time I left. You two take care now, right?'

She grabs a jacket and runs out of the house. Shortly afterwards, her extraordinary banger of a car springs noisily into action and rattles off.

'Good,' says Fridz. 'Now I'll show you how we're going to do it.'

Do it, thinks Konrad. He doesn't like the sound of this.

They have to do something, but why couldn't they just play *Crazy Bugs,* for example, and have a good laugh? Or they could curl up somewhere comfortable and tell each other mad stories. That'd be good fun too. But no – Fridz wants to do something. And obviously, he is supposed to go along with her.

Fridz is already on the stairs down to the basement.

'Coming,' says Konrad. He is talking mostly to himself, as if he is giving himself an order. Off you go, my dear Konrad. There is no going back. In for a penny, in for a pound. You've started, so you'll finish. And so on. Things that Mum and Dad must love saying, because they repeat them so often.

'You'll be amazed,' says Fridz, when they get to the basement. 'I have a new plan. And this time I've thought of everything. It can't go wrong.'

Famous last words! Konrad has heard this kind of thing before. 'It can't go wrong.' The thieves in his detective stories say this kind of thing regularly, just before they fall into the trap that the Sly Foxes gang of children have set. It's always the same. 'It can't go wrong' means roughly: 'Whatever we do now, it will all go up the spout.' It's just another way of saying it. And it's always the stupid ones who say it, the ones who are sure to come a cropper.

But that's what happens, thinks Konrad, when someone lets himself be persuaded into playing with a girl. Anyone who plays with a girl is destined to have to spend the rest of his life doing dreadfully embarrassing things. Rudolf the Red-Nosed Reindeer! They'd warned him at school, but unfortunately, they hadn't fully explained to him what the consequences would be.

By now, Fridz has opened the door into the store room where all the boxes are. She goes in, pulling Konrad behind her, and closes the door after them.

And there it is, the new plan. You can't miss it. Within a fraction of a second, Konrad knows exactly what she has in mind. He could not have dreamt up anything as bad as this.

'Well,' says Fridz. 'Deadly, isn't it?'

This word is not allowed in the Bantelmann family. But Konrad kind of knows that he shouldn't say that right now.

'Yes,' he says instead. 'Mad.' But what he means is, 'awful'.

On the other hand, you have to hand it to her. Fridz has really gone to a lot of trouble. On top of two other boxes, as if on a podium, stands a box like no other box the world has ever seen. That's what Fridz says anyway. And to emphasise this pronouncement, she lifts it up and displays it from all angles. And it is well worth looking at from every angle.

'Here,' she says, 'if you would like to take a look.'

On all four sides, the words OFFICIAL ANIMAL SHIPMENT are written in thick black marker and every letter has been framed first in red, than in yellow.

Low down on each side it says, in slightly smaller writing, so that it all fits in: THIS SHIPMENT IS FULLY LEGAL AND PERMITTED.

'Mad,' says Konrad. 'It can't go wrong.'

'But,' says Fridz, 'watch!'

She sticks her finger through a little hole and pulls open a flap that is about as big as a playing card. On the inside of the flap it says: SPECIAL RABBIT BREATHING HOLE.

'There are six of these altogether,' says Fridz. 'Exactly as it says in the instructions.'

What instructions? Konrad would like to ask, but he doesn't. Probably, in the spirit of the new code of conflict, it's best not to say anything at all for the moment.

'And now watch! It gets madder!'

Fridz indicates another flap on the top of the box, beside which is written: SPECIAL RABBIT FEEDING CHUTE. And a bit smaller: INSERT ONE CARROT HERE EVERY HOUR!

'Mad,' says Konrad. He can't think of anything else to say.

And although he probably shouldn't ask, he does ask. 'And how,' he says, 'ehh . . . how are you planning to carry it?'

'Well, how do you think!' Fridz taps her forehead to show how smart she is and how smart Konrad is not. 'Same as yesterday. We pack the rabbit into the box, we put the box on the trolley and then we pull the thing to the cow's house.'

Oh dear!

'Maybe,' says Konrad, 'maybe we could play some other trick on this Kristine?'

'Out of the question,' says Fridz. 'She has to get an allergy and she has to scratch herself to bits.'

Well, it was worth a try. Konrad thinks some more. And something does in fact occur to him, slowly but surely. 'But,' he says.

'Yes? But? Go on.'

'How are you going to get the rabbit into the flat?'

Fridz taps her forehead again. She really is feeling very smart today. 'The stupid cow works very close to her stupid cowshed. In a clothes shop. We'll go there, you'll stay outside and mind the giant, I'll go in and wangle the key out of her.'

'Hmm,' says Konrad. He knocks on the box. 'But if RABBIT is written all over it, then she won't open it.'

Bingo!

Fridz grins so broadly that the corners of her mouth nearly reach her ears.

'My mum,' she says, 'sometimes tells me how much smarter women are than men. And you know, my mum is not exactly on top of things right now, but stupid she is not.'

Fridz stands right in front of Konrad. 'Now,' she says very softly and very clearly, 'here comes the most ingenious part of my plan. I'm telling you, she won't notice a thing. We will go into the flat, we will take the bunny rabbit out of the box, and we will chase it all over the place so hard that it will shed thousands of its allergy hairs.'

Fridz turns around and pretends to be driving something in front of her.

'Shoo! Shoo!' she cries. 'Up on the sofa, you little pet. Into the bed. Turn around, roll a bit. Well done!' Then she stands so close to Konrad again that the tip of her nose is exactly one millimetre from the tip of Konrad's nose.

'You see?' she says. 'When the whole place is full of hairs, then we scarper, and nobody can lay a finger on us. So what do you say – ingenious or what?'

A rhetorical question.

'And where does this Kristine live?' asks Konrad quietly.

'Hmm,' says Fridz. She takes one step back. 'Not very far away. Do you know Gerhard's toy shop?'

Who wouldn't know Gerhard's toy shop!

'Near there.'

'What?' says Konrad.

To get to Gerhard's toy shop from The Dransfeld you'd have to go all the way into town and then a bit further. It could take hours on foot. Or, who knows, maybe even days.

'But,' says Konrad, 'but . . .'

'But what?' says Fridz.

'It's too far.'

'Too far? Too far!' There is no doubt about it, Fridz is getting shirty. 'That's the way scaredy people talk.'

'Suppose we took the bus?'

'You think we can get the box and the trolley onto a bus? Up those steep steps?'

No, if he is to be honest, Konrad doesn't really think so.

'A taxi?'

'Not a hope,' says Fridz. 'Taxi drivers don't take children.'

'How do you know that?'

Fridz rolls her eyes. 'Last week, Mum was in a spin and I wanted to go to her. I called a taxi, but the driver said 'only when accompanied by an adult'. And remember, we have this bunny box with us. That'd send the taxi driver into a spin too, and there'd be a right to-do.'

Yes, Konrad has to admit, that could well happen.

'Well, then. There's nothing else for it, is there?'

Or is there? Konrad thinks. If he doesn't come up with a good answer right away to this 'or is there' question, then he is going to have to pull this wretched trolley with the Flemish Giant box on it all the way through town. Or . . . well, then what? Or it's all over between him and this Fridz.

But she'll never be able to do it on her own. And if he lets her down now, then there is no code of conflict on earth that can reconcile them. Then Konrad Bantelmann would be forever free of his red-haired, terrifying, nerve-shattering, catastrophe-inducing Friederike. But for some reason, Konrad doesn't want that to happen, so he says something outrageous. He says, 'I could ask my father.'

'What?'

'I could ask my father to drive us. We have a Passat. We could put the box in the back. For sure.'

'What?' says Fridz. 'Are you stupid?' She wrings her hands. 'It can't be! There has to be a law against people being that stupid.'

'How d'you mean?'

'How do I mean? Do you really think your father would drive us if he knew what we are doing with this rabbit?'

'No,' says Konrad. And then he says something even more outrageous. He says: 'We'd have to keep him in the dark about that.'

'Wow,' says Fridz. And then again: 'Wow!'

Then she says nothing for at least ten seconds, which for her is an extraordinarily long time. She is obviously impressed. In the end, she says, 'And what were you thinking of telling him, if he asks?'

'Hmm. Maybe that the rabbit is sick. That it has to go to the vet. Something like that.'

'Oh, boy,' says Fridz. 'You're a right one. Professor Superclever and his great plan.'

That's a bit sharp, but the way she says it, it doesn't sound sharp at all. It sounds rather complimentary.

'And you really think he'd believe you?'

Konrad shrugs his shoulders and says nothing. This looks good, but he doesn't feel one bit good. Though 'not one bit good' isn't quite the right expression. He actually feels as sick as a dog. Good heavens, what has he suggested? He's going to get his father mixed up in the whole rabbit revenge thing, without his even noticing. Which would mean that he, Konrad Bantelmann, would have to . . . tell lies!

'Wow,' says Fridz again. 'Wow, wow, wow. That's really something!' Obviously, she no longer doubts that this plan is going to work.

Konrad has started to doubt if he is still upright, considering how the ground is swaying under his feet.

'Let's play *Crazy Bugs* and afterwards we can go to the canal,' says Fridz.

Oh, sure, to the canal. That's just great, another thing he is not supposed to do.

The Great Divorce Test

An hour later, the two of them are sitting there, where they sat two days ago, at the forbidden canal. They are letting their legs hang down over the water and Fridz is throwing little stones in again.

But one important thing is quite different from how it was two days ago. Two days ago they had just woken up Fridz's mum, who is so unhappy that she sometimes takes sleeping tablets so that she can get some sleep and forget her unhappiness. And then Konrad – completely coincidentally and unintentionally – had given Fridz the appalling idea of sending an allergy rabbit to her father's girlfriend. Because she was so angry and so sad.

But when Konrad gives a secret sidelong glance at her now, she looks fairly happy, even though she is saying nothing and is just looking out over the canal. Since this appalling allergy rabbit project started, she hasn't been as sad and as angry as she was two days ago here at the canal. Cutting – yes, she's been that all along. Unbelievably sharp. And cross. Even super-cross. But being sharp and being cross are easier to take than being sad, both for oneself and for other people. And this makes Konrad think that maybe this rabbit idea is not so harebrained as he had thought at first.

However, what he himself set in motion an hour ago in the basement of number 28b is total lunacy. His father would drive them into town, he'd said, and the law-abiding Konrad Bantelmann, of all people, is to lie himself blue in the face to get him to do it. Was that really the only option? Konrad wonders now. Would it not have been a thousand times better to pull the awful, squeaky trolley through half the town, rather than let himself in for all these lies he is going to have to tell? Probably yes. But there's no going back now.

'Hey, you,' says Konrad.

'Yeah?'

'How's your mother?'

'All right,' says Fridz. 'This afternoon, she has to go to the bank. And this morning we were at the solicitor's. For the seven hundred thousandth time. They want to organise an interim access order.'

'A what?'

'In-ter-im ac-cess or-der. It says how often my dear father is allowed to visit me and what we can do together.'

'Oh?' says Konrad. 'Is there such a thing?'

'Obviously.' Fridz pulls up her legs and sits cross-legged. 'That's why I had to go too. I'm allowed to make suggestions. Here, listen.'

She pulls a piece of paper out of her back pocket and opens it out. Then she reads out loud: ' "It is hereby arranged and ordered that Herr Matthias Frenke picks up his only daughter Friederike Luise every Friday at 4 p.m. from her home and then immediately takes her to see the film of her choice. Before the cinema, she gets a bucket of candied popcorn and afterwards a pizza with everything she wants on it, including jelly babies and licorice snakes. Finally, she may watch television until her eyes close and Herr Frenke must then carry her to bed, without waking her." What do you make of that?'

Konrad nearly said 'deadly'. But only nearly. What he actually says is, 'Mad.'

'It goes on. Listen! "On Saturday mornings, Herr Frenke must let his only daughter Friederike Luise sleep as long as she wants, and subsequently he is to make her pancakes for breakfast with sugar and syrup. And his stupid girlfriend Kristine is not to be present at breakfast or to try to paw her disgustingly."'

'Wow!' says Konrad. 'And they've really allowed all that?'

'I don't know,' says Fridz.

'What d'you mean, you don't know?'

'I didn't read it to them.' Fridz folds the paper and puts it back in her pocket.

'Why not?'

'Because it would make my mum even sadder.' She punches Konrad in the shoulder. 'You should be there sometime when we go to the solicitor. It's dreadful, I'm telling you. First, Mum is totally nervous. Really panicking. Sometimes she sits down suddenly somewhere and starts crying. A few times, she's even been crying in the car. When we're actually at the solicitor's, she's totally cool and she talks to the man for hours, all about payments.'

'About payments?'

'Yes, how much Dad has to pay her, how much he has to

pay for me and how much he has to save so that I can go to university. Pure money stuff. And then,' Fridz starts throwing stones into the canal, 'then, if it's about the house, that's the worst. Because the stupid house doesn't belong to either Mum or Dad. The stupid house belongs to the bank, and Mum says if we don't watch like a hawk and let Dad just do as he pleases, then we'll have to move out again within a few months.'

'Why's that?' Konrad is horrified.

'Dunno,' says Fridz. 'In any case, Mum and the solicitor talk for hours about the house. And about payments. And the more they talk about payments, the sadder Mum gets. As long as we're at the solicitor's, she's fine. But on the way home in the car, by the first traffic light at the latest, she starts wailing again. All the way home. Then she stops the car in front of the garage and stumbles out of it to the door and says, "Crap house." And then . . . '

'What then?'

Fridz says nothing for a moment. Then she starts throwing stones into the canal with both hands at the same time.

'Dunno,' she says. 'Something. Anyway, she's always super super bad after that. And if I read out a page like that, then she would definitely be even worse.'

'I understand,' says Konrad.

'You understand nothing,' says Fridz. But she doesn't say it sharply at all. She rubs her hands together and lets her legs hang down again. 'You wouldn't want anyone to be able to understand the first thing about such a heap of crap.'

Konrad has taken a very small stone and now he lets it fall down into the canal by his legs. The stone goes *splish*.

'Would you think,' he says, 'that my parents might separate too?'

'Haven't a clue!'

'But I thought you'd know about things like that.'

Fridz laughs. 'I don't know a thing about your parents,' she says. 'I have a hard enough time understanding my own.'

'Hmm,' says Konrad. 'But your whole family is divorced. You must know more about it than I do.'

'Okay,' says Fridz. 'If you say so.' She grins again, as only she can grin. 'So let's do a test.'

'What kind of a test?'

'A big divorce test. I'll ask you a few questions, and if you answer most of them with yes, then your parents are going to get divorced soon.'

'Oh,' says Konrad. He hadn't expected this. 'How many questions?'

'Well,' says Fridz, 'I think maybe five. Agreed?'

Konrad pulls his legs up and wraps his arms around his knees. He's feeling a bit uneasy. Five questions – that means, he mustn't answer yes more than twice. Otherwise his parents will get divorced.

'Agreed,' he says. 'Get started!'

'Away we go!' Fridz bites her lower lip. 'Question number one: Have you built a house lately?'

'You know that!'

'So, the answer to the first question is yes.'

'Yes, but –'

The first question and Konrad is already up to his neck in it.

But Fridz is right. Franzkarl Findouter and his wife Evelyn have also got divorced, just after they had built a house. And the Bantelmann parents had squabbled a lot during the building of the house. About such ridiculously unimportant things as where the second washbasin should go in the bathroom, what kind of tiles should they lay in the hall, whether the drainpipe should be round or square, and so on and so forth.

Konrad says 'But–' again, but he can't think of anything more to say.

'Yeah, well, but,' says Fridz. 'One nil to divorce. Second question: Do your parents fight every Sunday morning at breakfast until one of them takes something off the table and throws it on the floor?'

'No!' cries Konrad very quickly and very loudly. Not every Sunday morning – you certainly could not say that. In any case, Peter – and sometimes Konrad himself – is responsible for throwing things on the floor. A definite no.

'One all,' says Fridz. 'Third question: does your mum stand in front of her wardrobe sometimes and say, "I really don't know who I'm putting all this stuff on for?"'

Konrad thinks. His mother does sometimes stand for a long time in front of her wardrobe. But she always says something quite different. She says, 'I have absolutely nothing to wear.' If Dad hears this, first he laughs for a quarter of an hour, and then he kisses Mum and calls her so many funny names that she laughs too. Konrad tells Fridz all this.

'Yeah, yeah,' she says. 'That'll do. So, it's a no. That makes it two to one against divorce. Fourth question.' Fridz seems to have to think. 'Fourth questionn,' she says again, very slowly. But then it comes to her: 'Have your parents considered taking separate holidays?'

Ouch! Konrad can feel his ears going red. His parents did think of that, this very year. Dad suggested that Mum might take him and Peter for a week to the sea, and while they were away, Dad could get a few little jobs finished around the house. That way they would save on the double: the money for Dad's hotel and the money they would otherwise pay to get the jobs done on the house. A sensible suggestion. But Mum was very much against it. And in the end, when Dad came back from the bank in a very bad mood, they decided that this year they'd all stay at home, in order to save even more money.

'All the same,' says Fridz. 'That counts as a yes. Whether or not they actually did it. It's enough that they discussed doing it. I'm telling you, that's the beginning of the end. So now it's two all.'

Fridz raises a hand. 'In other words, ladies and gentlemen,' she says, like a ringmaster who is announcing the number of lions the lion-tamer is going to produce, 'Konrad Bantelmann now faces the final and decisive question in the Great Divorce Test. Drum roll, please, orchestra!' And she makes a noise that is supposed to sound like a rumble of drums.

That's enough, thinks Konrad. If only he hadn't let himself in for this test!

'Right,' says Fridz, stretching the word right out. 'Riiiiiiiight.'

'Oh, get on with it,' says Konrad. It has to happen quickly or he will get even more jumpy.

'Right. Fifth question: do you get too many presents?'

'I beg your pardon?'

What kind of a question is that? Nobody in the world gets too many presents! No – that is impossible. That goes against the laws of nature, Dad would say. And Konrad says something like that now.

'D'you think?' says Fridz. 'Take me, for example. I get too many presents.'

'Seriously?'

'Completely seriously. From my dad. I get something every time he comes to see me.'

'But that's super!' Maybe, Konrad thinks, Fridz is mad after all.

'Yeah?' she says. 'D'you reckon? Then start wishing that your parents will be very unhappy together. Because if they are unhappy together, then they start thinking whether it might not be better for them to get divorced. But when they think about divorce, then they get a bad conscience. Because there's you, and you have nothing to do with their unhappiness. "The poor child!" they think. And out of pure guilt, they give you a whole toy shop full of presents.'

'Ach,' says Konrad.

'Ach is right. And then when they really do separate, it gets even crazier. Do you really think I got *Crazy Bugs 3* because I am such a sweet and well-behaved little girl and always eat up my porridge?'

Konrad would rather not answer.

'So you see. And in case you're interested in what you get when your parents get divorced, you can take a look any day at my soft toy collection, which my dear runaway father has bestowed upon me, so that I won't be all alone with my mum and his stupid bunny.'

'But there aren't any soft toys in your room,' says Konrad. He's been in her room, and he's never seen a single soft toy in it.

'They're in the basement,' says Fridz. 'Near the bins. I go down once a day and torture them with needles and scissors. You should hear how they scream for help. There's this stupid green turtle; he shouts the loudest. You have to stuff your ears when he starts.'

'Is that really true?'

'Yeah,' says Fridz. 'Or maybe I've been telling lies. Maybe it's the funny little beaver that howls the loudest. Or this totally outrageous purple dinosaur with disgusting yellow spots. Or one of the super-sweet little woolly mice that you can arrange nicely in a row on a very long skewer.'

Konrad thinks of his own mouse, with the problematic name of Mattchoo. Just as well he has never mentioned it to Fridz.

'You'd do a thing like that?' he says.

'Sure,' says Fridz. 'Not always, but often. I call it woolly mouse kebab. And if the creatures shout, then I turn them over an open flame, until they are crisp on the outside and juicy on the inside. That's good fun.'

'Ha ha,' goes Konrad. But this 'Ha ha' is nothing like a real laugh.

'Just pay attention,' says Fridz. 'If your parents are getting divorced, then you'll get up to five thousand sweet little cars. You could smash them up good and proper between two bricks. That would probably be good fun too.'

'But,' says Konrad, 'my parents are not getting divorced. Have you forgotten? The score is three two.'

'Oh?' says Fridz. 'You don't get too many presents? Honestly?'

'Yes,' says Konrad. 'I mean, no, I really don't get too many presents. Dad has even gone so far as to say I will be getting fewer things, because we all have to save.'

'Okay,' says Fridz. 'I get it.'

'So that's three two against divorce.'

'Agreed.' Fridz stands up and brushes something off her trousers. 'But I'm telling you, three two is tight enough. Four one would have been better. But listen, when are you going to ask your father if he will drive us?'

Oh, right. Konrad hadn't given it a thought all this time. Instead, he'd been worrying about what might happen to his parents in the unforeseeable future. Could it be, he wonders, that you worry about one thing so that you can forget about something else?

That sounds kind of stupid. On the other hand, he's learnt from experience that things don't refrain from happening just because they are stupid. On the contrary, it's the stupid things that seem to happen without fail. For example, falling down and hurting your knee. And especially knocking over the chocolate. Things like that can't get enough of happening.

'Hey,' says Fridz. 'Are you dreaming? I asked you something.'

'Yeah, yeah,' says Konrad. 'Today. I'll ask him today. And tomorrow we'll be at your door. Shall we say nine o'clock?'

'Nine o'clock sharp!' says Fridz. 'Good. Henri will still be asleep. But not a minute later.'

Then she makes a gesture that means 'come on, let's go home'. Konrad stands obediently up, brushes something off his trousers too and the two of them start to walk along by the canal.

'I hope you know that it's all up to you,' says Fridz, as they come to the little path that leads from the canal into The Dransfeld. 'If you let the cat out of the bag and your father finds out what we're really up to, then we're up the creek for all eternity.' She stops and grabs Konrad by the arms. 'Do you know what I will do then?'

Konrad shakes his head.

'Then I will give my mum a present of a special roast rabbit cookbook.'

Konrad laughs, although he is not really in the mood for laughing.

'Rabbit steamed in a box,' he says.

And Fridz laughs too. 'Or rabbit braised in a puff-pastry trolley. An old family recipe of the master chef Friederike von Roastaroma.'

'Very good,' says Konrad. 'And for dessert, we'll serve Flemish Giant compote with ketchup and mayonnaise.'

Fridz laughs so much that she can hardly keep upright.

'And to drink, our head waiter Mr Bantelmann recommends a first class hutch-bottled Pinot Fur.'

'Stop!' screeches Fridz, and because she really cannot keep upright any longer, she falls on her bottom. 'My ribcage!' she squeals between roars of laughter. 'It's bursting.'

'Did you say rabbit cage?' says Konrad. 'Fur from the rabbit cage is very good for a stiff neck, you gather it up and you put it under your feet at night.'

But then Fridz really can't breathe any more, so Konrad stops making jokes about eating rabbit, because otherwise she will never make it home.

The Planet Klimbambium

No sooner has Konrad entered number 17a than suddenly the laughter wears right off. Because, somehow, he has to persuade his dad to actively support this utterly mad allergy project against Kristine Crisis. Konrad still hasn't the foggiest idea how he is going to do this. He retreats quickly to his room, so that he has as much time as possible before dinner to think about it. And so that he doesn't forget any good ideas, he writes down everything that occurs to him in his Dransfeld notebook. A few seconds later, he has actually got three plans.

Plan number one seems the simplest. He says, 'Hello, Dad. A small request from your elder son. Could you please drive Friederike and her rabbit to the vet? The creature has some kind of fungus, and has to be supervised by the doctor for a few days. They have to find out if it's infectious. Can you do that for us? Great. Thanks!'

Sounds really easy, this plan, but it has the small disadvantage that it is a lie from beginning to end. And Konrad Bantelmann is not a world champion liar. On the contrary. The probability that he will stumble and stutter as soon as he starts to tell a lie is extraordinarily high, and with it the probability that he will make a hash of the whole rabbit project.

Plan number two sounds a bit more complicated. This is

how it goes: 'Hello, Dad. I want to ask you something. Friederike, you know who I mean, I've told you about her, she wants to give someone a surprise present, a rabbit, actually, but it's supposed to be a big secret. Anyway, she has no way of transporting it, because she hasn't got a dad any more, and so she's asked me to ask you if you would give her a lift tomorrow. You'll do it? Ace. Friederike will be delighted. Thanks a lot.'

Not bad, eh? That'd be about half true and half a lie. Because it's kind of right, if you overlook the fact that the nasty intention behind the project is concealed. At any rate, there's a reasonable chance that Konrad won't start stumbling and stammering. On the other hand, Konrad is unfortunately equipped with a rather curious dad – and he'd be sure to question such an interesting but clearly gappy story: who's supposed to be surprised, and why, and why with a rabbit, and how exactly is it supposed to happen? And so on and so forth. In a word, nothing but questions, and questions that Konrad must not under any circumstances answer, if the enormous lie at the centre of this story is not to come out and the whole project to go sky high.

That leaves plan number three. This was the last one Konrad thought of. At first, he was very pleased with it. For plan number three is simply to tell the truth. Like this: 'Hello, Dad. Have you got five minutes? Thanks. I've got myself into a bit of a weird situation. See, there's this Friederike, you know, this mad girl from number 28b. Well, her father has left home, because he has a girlfriend, just like Franzkarl Findouter – and Friederike is so cross about it that she wants to send a rabbit to his girlfriend, who, as it happens, is also called Kristine. The idea is that the girlfriend will get an allergy (take deep breath) – right, and as luck would have it, in a fit of weakness, I promised that you would transport this rabbit to the girlfriend, and this is the thing, see, no way is Friederike under any circumstances to find out that you know what she's planning, which is why you must not only drive us into town, but also behave as if you think we're just taking the rabbit to the vet (another deep breath) or something like that – so, now it's out. Daddy dear, please do it to get me out of this fix, because otherwise I will look like the dumbest cluck in the whole world, and you wouldn't like that, would you? Well, anyway, that's what I wanted to say.'

That's how it would be, everything nice and honest. Here I am, Dad, there's nothing else I can say. Help me – or leave me in the worst situation I've ever been in in my whole life. Fantastic! And honest Konrad would have nothing else to do but wait to see what His Majesty, Dad von Bantelmann of The Dransfeld will decide in the case in question.

However, plan number three has one small, one very tiny defect: plan number three is cowardly. Cowardly through and through. And not only that – it would be a betrayal. Because, if you say to a friend, I'll help you and I'll keep it a secret, and then if you go and tell someone else the whole story, then you've betrayed your friend. Especially if the someone else is your own dad.

That's the way it is. There's no getting away from it. Konrad Bantelmann is in a fix. No matter what he does, it'll be wrong. Plan number one or plan number two: he lies to his dad. Plan number three: he betrays Fridz. There is no way out of this dilemma. And that's what it says in black, black letters under the three plans in The Dransfeld notebook, when Mum calls him to dinner.

People who are in a fix like this are either very noisy or very quiet. Konrad Bantelmann is, as you might expect, very quiet – so quiet that after a while it starts to needle people.

'Is something wrong?' asks Mum.

'No,' says Konrad. That's the first lie.

'Were you with your new girlfriend today?' Dad wants to know.

'Yes,' says Konrad.

Is that a lie too? Maybe, on account of the not entirely unproblematic, or to put it another way, on account of the very dangerous word, *girlfriend*? No, Konrad clenches his teeth and decides it's not a lie.

'So?' says Dad. 'How did it go today? You two seem pretty inseparable.'

'Hmm,' says Konrad. If Dad only knew how right he is! At any rate, the fate of Konrad Bantelmann is currently inseparably linked to Fridz's rabbit box.

'They're in love,' says Peter.

Would you listen to that! Konrad had never before so fervently wished his brother on Mars or, better still, on Jupiter. But by a great effort of will, and with bright red ears, he manages not to say anything. The subject is just too sensitive.

'Anything else interesting to tell us?' asks Dad, in this tone of voice that means Konrad had better watch out if he doesn't want to make a total mess of everything. A bad atmosphere at dinner would really be the last straw.

'Well,' says Konrad, pretending to think hard. Actually he is thinking hard. What can he tell Dad that will stop him asking questions?

This might do: 'Friederike,' says Konrad, 'she's got *Crazy Bugs 4* now. It's class. When you're on level seven, then you haven't just got ten nets and stuff like that, but you have this fully automatic catching device and this is what it looks like: there's this big arm, it's on a tower or a mast or something. And it's about this long.' Konrad indicates diagonally across the table. 'And if you click on this spot with the mouse, and at the same time you press the Enter key, then –'

'Thank you,' says Dad. He feels quite sufficiently informed, he says, and is pleased about his son's participation in the development of computer technology. Then he goes into the kitchen, gets a bottle of beer and doesn't ask any more questions. Which is fine.

But Konrad doesn't ask any questions either. Which is not so fine. Because dinner is coming to an end, without any problems and without a bad atmosphere having descended – but also without a solution to Konrad's larger-than-life rabbit problem.

At eight sharp, Peter and Konrad wriggle themselves into position beside Dad, to hear the next instalment of the forest snake story.

'We were,' says Dad, and Peter is being so careful not to kick him in the stomach that he forgets to breathe, 'at the bad quarrel that the two half-snakes, Ana and Basis, were having about what they should do next in the matter of the mysterious crystal.'

'Poooo,' goes Peter, who has almost suffocated. Luckily, only almost. Unfortunately, however, he kicks Dad pretty hard in the side as he takes a breath.

'Oops,' he says.

'Not to worry,' says Dad. He says he has got so used to being kicked while storytelling that at this stage he would probably not be able to think of anything to tell if he isn't kicked a bit first. It's pretty normal by now. Most people have to be kicked to make them think of something.

'Ha ha,' says Dad.

It's this so-called irony. Konrad knows this, but he chooses to say nothing.

'Well, then,' says Dad instead, 'as it happens the sun is shining again, which means that somehow life must go on. The members of the expedition spend the whole next day debating how the mysterious crystal is to be brought to the great resarch laboratory. It's up to the two forest snakes now to step smartly up to the mark. They don't know what has to be done, but they know that time is getting tight, and that whatever it is must be done quickly.'

Dad pauses. 'Just like real life.'

'Go on,' says Peter.

'Very well.' Dad sighs. 'The two half-snakes wait until the dark, tropical night falls over the crystal and over the expedition, and then they set out, separately, on secret voyages of discovery. Who can remember what Basis wanted?'

A test question. Konrad really has had enough of those

today. 'To find out what this whole thing is about, this thing with the mysterious crystal,' he says all the same.

'Correct,' says Dad. 'Very well remembered. And for this reason he slithers to the point on the crystal, where the explorers – completely in vain – had broken off a piece. It is very still in the jungle night. As still as if the forest animals were holding their breath in suspense.'

Peter holds his own breath again.

'Hey,' says Dad, 'not you, the forest animals. Or are you a forest animal?'

'No,' says Peter and breathes again.

'Well,' says Dad. 'And the forest snake Basis has hardly reached the tip of the crystal when something extraordinary and exciting happens. As he creeps up to it in the dark, he touches the exposed crystal. For the first time in all these years, he touches its smooth, reflective surface, and immediately the crystal starts to flash and to glow. It flashes and glows red and blue and green and yellow deep down into the depths where it is still buried deep in the earth.'

'Oh,' says Peter. 'Is it hot too?'

'No,' says Dad.

'But if it's glowing like that . . . '

'No,' says Dad again. 'It is definitely not hot. It does flash and glow, but it is not hot, lukewarm at the most, and also it gives off a soft, ringing sound.'

Peter lifts Lackilug the mouse up so that the little bell around its neck tinkles.

'A soft ringing sound,' says Dad, 'not a tinkling sound. It's different.'

Peter stuffs Lackilug the mouse back down under the covers. He says something that no one can understand. Possibly he is offended.

'In any case,' says Dad, 'Basis gets a shock like he never got before. But before he can even think of fleeing, the most astonishing thing of all happens. What do you think it might be?'

Of course the boys haven't a clue.

'Well, listen up, now!' says Dad. 'By some miracle, and entirely soundlessly, a door opens in the tip of the crystal, at precisely the spot where the forest snake touched it, a little door that until this moment was not to be seen. A door just big enough for a normal adult forest snake to slip through without any trouble. And as if driven by a secret power, Basis the forest snake does indeed slip, quivering with excitement, in through the circular forest snake door and into the inside of the crystal.

'Whereupon, no sooner has the tip of the tail of the snake gone through it, than the door closes over, so that no one can see where it once was. Well, what do you say to that?'

The boys say nothing at all.

'Hmm,' says Dad. 'And now things really start happening. The forest snake slips through a long, dark channel, spiralling and twirling continuously, deeper and deeper into the crystal. It penetrates so far that it thinks it's on a journey to the centre of the earth and is totally lost – and then at last a hatch opens and the forest snake flies another bit through the empty air and then lands gently, on the most astonishingly soft floor of a large room, which is very light and seems to be made completely of glass.'

Dad waits to see if the boys are going to say anything, but they say nothing.

'So, as I said, it's very bright in this room, and all around the walls and also on the ceiling there are all these buttons and switches and monitors and as many kinds of technical gadgets as you can possibly imagine. And there, just at that moment, as he is contemplating all the buttons and switches and all the bits and bobs, it suddenly becomes clear to the forest snake what the whole thing is. And what also becomes clear to him is who he himself really is!'

Dad pauses. You can practically touch his satisfaction with his story this evening. His satisfaction with his story hovers, in a manner of speaking, like a great, red, billowing kite in the air directly over Peter's bed.

'Well?' says Dad. 'What do you think? What has the forest snake discovred inside the crystal?'

Not a clue. What could a forest snake discover inside a crystal with lots of buttons? That you can have strange experiences at night in the forest? That you shouldn't go into places just because you fit into them? Or what?

If he were to be quite honest, Konrad is not all that terribly interested this evening in the doings of this half-snake. He has his own worries. And his main worry is that he only has about ten minutes to ask his father the question of questions. Because in ten minutes, the light will go out and then it's not just good night, dear forest snake, but also, good night, not-so-dear rabbit project. And goodbye, dear Fridz!

'Well,' says Dad, 'wait till you hear! First of all, the forest snake has this great feeling of familiarity and security. He doesn't know why, but he feels quite at home, and as if everything is fine. It lasts a few minutes and then he begins to remember that the mysterious crystal is really a spaceship from the planet Klimbambium, and he himself is the transmogrified Klimbambionic chief astronaut Nil Ambstronk.'

'Hey!' says Peter. He likes this story. Out of sheer excitement, he presses Lackilug hard against his nose.

'Yes,' says Dad. 'And just as if he is waking out of a long, dreamy sleep, this Klimbambionic chief astronaut Nil Ambstronk also remembers that four hundred and thirty-seven Klimbambionic years ago, the spaceship Klimbine 9, on a routine monitoring operation, came hurtling through the universe onto, of all places, Planet Earth, and drilled its way down into the jungle floor.'

Lackilug the mouse does a very good imitation of the sound of the impact.

'Very good,' says Dad. 'May I continue?'

He may.

'Right. So, Nil Ambstronk and his co-pilot Eddi Aldi survived the landing, but Klimbine 9 was beyond repair, because some important materials didn't exist on Earth. And besides, they had lost contact, so they couldn't call for help. For this reason, the two astronauts, heavy of heart, had decided to have themselves transformed by their transmutator into the double forest snake Anabasis and to stand guard over the spaceship in this form, to make sure that it did not fall into the wrong hands. So now what do you say?'

The great red kite of Dad's satisfaction rustles softly, but proudly, in the breeze.

'Hmm,' says Peter. He's never said that before in his whole life.

Dad is a little perplexed.

'It's a damned good story,' he says. 'Or isn't it?'

'Oh, yes, sure,' says Konrad quickly. There must on no account be a bad atmosphere.

And the best way to prevent such a thing would be to ask a few particularly clever questions.

So he says 'Ah,' in a questioning kind of way, though he hasn't a notion what to ask. But then he thinks of something. 'How come the forest snake didn't know before now who he is and where he comes from?'

'Ah,' says Dad now, also in a questioning tone.

Oh dear, thinks Konrad, hoping this question wasn't too clever. That'd be stupid!

But he's in luck.

'This is the way it was,' says Dad. 'Nil Ambstronk and Eddi Aldo –'

'Aldi,' says Peter out from under Lackilug the mouse.

'Pardon, Aldi – they had programmed the transmutator in such a way that they would not only be transformed into forest snakes, but they would forget everything – except their mission to guard the crystal. And the reason for this was so that they wouldn't try, out of sheer homesickness for their home planet Klimbambion – '

'Klimbambium,' says Lackilug the mouse in Peter's voice.

'Sorry, I mean, so that they wouldn't get desperately unhappy or go mad, out of homesickness for their home planet Klimbambium. Better to be two fairly limited forest snakes, they thought, than two homeless, unhappy and bored astronauts. Obvious enough, right?'

Sure thing.

'And why is nobody allowed near the spaceship?' asks Konrad.

'Aha!' cries Dad. 'The question of questions! For the very simple and pressing reason that the profoundly advanced technology of the Klimbambions must on no account fall into the hands of the essentially irrational and belligerent Earthlings. It's unbelievable the kind of tomfoolery such people might get up to with it.'

Dad is glowing with pleasure at how well he has winkled this surprising development into the forest snake story. He's glowing so hard that Konrad is going to have to shift a bit aside so as not to get burnt by him. This would be a good moment, he thinks, to raise the subject of the business with the rabbit. But how, exactly, should he do it? How is he going to effect a transition from the irrationality of humanity in general to the single, totally absurd project of one mad red-haired girl?

But then it becomes suddenly clear that there is no point in thinking about it any more, because, although it is not yet quite a quarter past eight, Dad has obviously decided to finish the current instalment of the story with this sparkling Klimbambium business.

Still in the best of moods, he sits up with a single movement, thumps and tickles Peter and Konrad a little, wishes them both a good night and goes out onto the landing.

'Lights out in five minutes!' he cries, and then his steps are to be heard on the stairs.

And Konrad still hasn't asked.

Bigomil A. Deceiver

Peter and Konrad do put the lights out after five minutes. Their two mice, however, are still pretty lively and they chat away in the dark from one room to the other.

At first it's all about the latest instalment of the forest snake story. Peter's mouse, Lackilug, did not, apparently, quite understand what had happened. Maybe he is just pretending to be more stupid than he actually is. All the same, Mattchoo tells him the whole transformation story again.

'And besides,' says Matchoo in his squeaky voice – it sounds like 'beshaids' – 'besides, you probably can't really expect to be able to understand absolutely everything in the story. But we do at least know that these forest snake astronauts come from the planet Klimbambium, where everything is much more modern, and therefore also much more complicated, than things are on Earth.' And while he is at it, Mattchoo the mouse explains to Lackilug the mouse a few other complicated and uncommonly advanced gadgets that they have on the planet Klimbambium.

For example, the totally automatic car wash, except not for cars but for people, where even your toenails get cut automatically and it doesn't hurt a bit; the remote-controlled schoolbooks that you only need to put under your pillow at night and in the morning you know everything that's in them; the eating machines with flavour-changers that cook roast pork with red cabbage and dumplings that tastes like fresh fruit jelly with vanilla sauce; and a few other things that make life easier.

Lackilug eventually falls asleep, listening to these descriptions, and Konrad can hear Peter snoring gently. Shortly afterwards, Mattchoo the mouse also falls asleep. Only one person is still awake: Konrad Bantelmann. And he can't even think about sleep. Because if he can't work up the courage to ask his dad to render a particular service, then he may as well stay in bed tomorrow morning and pull the covers over his head. And the next day too. In fact, he can't ever put in an appearance again anywhere in the whole Dransfeld, and especially not anywhere near number 28b. And because that's the way it is – or rather, because that's the way it can't be allowed to be – the same Konrad Bantelmann climbs quietly out of his bed at twenty-five to nine. Very quietly, so as not to wake Mattchoo, Lackilug or Peter, he leaves the room. Just as quietly, holding his breath, he goes down the stairs until, very quietly, he reaches the closed living-room door.

He can feel his heart beating. He can even hear it beating. And before his parents on the other side of the living-room door also hear it beating, he knocks on the door.

'Yes?' says someone from inside.

In Konrad goes, and now here he is in the living room, where Dad is lying on the sofa, and Mum is sitting in the armchair, each with a book on their lap, and both of them looking at him as if he were the Principal Boy in a pantomime or as if he'd appeared at Easter in a diving suit and wished them a Happy Christmas.

'Hello,' says Konrad.

'Hello,' say his parents. They wonder if there is something so urgent that it can't wait until morning.

'Well, yes there is,' says Konrad. 'I can't sleep.' At least that much is not a word of a lie.

'Why not?'

'Because . . . because . . . ' Hell! He'll have to say it. He must. Even if it costs him his head. He must!

'Because I don't know what happens next in the story.'

Well done! Konrad Bantelmann – the world's greatest living coward. The next thing, they'll put him in a freak show, so that people can take a good look at him, a euro a go.

'Well!' says Dad.

'No!' says Konrad quickly. He's thinking so hard that any minute now steam is going to come spurting out of his ears.

'That's not it. I've been thinking how the story might go on. But I don't quite know if I've got it right. And that's why I can't sleep.'

'Hmm,' says Dad. 'Maybe you could tell us, and then we could see if it's right or not.'

'Well,' says Konrad. A great way to start a story!

What was it that Dad had said recently? Most people have to be kicked before they can think anything up. Konrad finally understands what he meant.

'Da-ad ,' he says. 'Remember Dr Deceiver?'

'Of course,' says Dad. 'Bigomil A. Deceiver, the unimaginative, underhanded, conniving would-be explorer.'

'Yes,' says Konrad. 'I mean, no. I think, actually, we have been unfair to him.'

'Really?' says Dad. 'That sounds interesting. In what way have we been unfair to him?'

Konrad sits in the little armchair and draws his feet up under his bottom.

'This is the way it was,' he says. 'Deceiver wanted to cut off a bit of the crystal.'

'Which Anabasis the – at the time still double – forest snake wanted to stop him from doing.'

'Correct. And we thought, he wants the piece of the crystal so that he can be the one to win the Nobble Prize for the best discovery.'

'Right,' says Dad.

'No, that's not right!' says Konrad and his voice sounds now almost like the politicians on the television. 'I know now that it was all totally different from what we thought.'

'Well, you surprise me,' says Dad. 'So, how was it then?'

'Maybe you won't believe it,' says Konrad. 'But in reality, Bigomil Deceiver is also an astronaut from the planet Klimbambium.'

'Oho!' says Dad. 'And what's his real name?'

'Oh,' says Konrad. A good question. Which is in urgent need of an answer.

'Darnok Retep,' he says quickly. 'That's his name, Darnok Retep. He was turned into the scientist Bigomil Deceiver on the planet Klimbambium and he has secretly been entrusted with the task of protecting the spaceship. That's why he followed the scientists over the Obernoko.'

'Hmm,' says Dad. 'But –'

No buts! Konrad is on a roll now. 'And do you know,' he says, 'when we thought he wanted to cut a piece out of the crystal, he was really looking for the entrance, the one that Basis the half-snake found.'

That fits. Konrad is very proud of himself.

'Well,' says Dad. 'But it's the forest snakes who are charged with protecting the spaceship.'

'Ye-ah,' says Konrad. There's no stopping him now. 'But unfortunately, the astronauts, Ambstronk and Aldi, have been unable to communicate with HQ on Klimbambium to let them know what form they have taken, and so they think – they have thought for four hundred and thirty-seven Klimbambionic years – that the spaceship is totally unprotected.'

'Sounds logical,' says Dad.

Logical? It sounds fantastic! Konrad has never before found the forest snake story as good as he finds it now.

'Yes,' he says. 'That's the way it is. Sometimes you think that people are only fooling around or even that they are doing something really bad, and then in the end you find out that they meant well all along.'

'Ah,' say his parents.

Konrad is really flying now. 'The forest snake, for example, should have just let Deceiver, I mean Darnok, get on with it, because he had this whole plan to get the valuable spaceship back to the planet Klimbambium.'

'Well, my goodness,' says Dad. 'That was stupid.'

'Wasn't it just! If the forest snake had kept its nose out

of things, then all the problems might have been solved.'
Konrad says this in a very reproachful tone of voice. 'Because
you see, Deceiver is a very reliable man, the best spaceship-
retrieval expert they've got. He's done it on several planets
before. And of course he has everything that is needed to repair the spaceship.'

'Well then,' says Dad. His eyes are squeezed up and his
forehead is all rumpled. 'That's pretty bad. Because as far as
I am aware, Ana the forest snake is now slithering into the
tent of Bigomil Deceiver – pardon me, of . . . '

'Darnok Retep.'

'Thank you. Because he is the very person that she wants
to put into a deep sleep with her paralysing bite. So now
what?'

'Oh, good heavens,' says Konrad. That would put the two
spaceship rescue teams out of business for good.

'Exactly,' says Dad with a grin.

'But that doesn't happen.'

'Why not?'

'Because,' says Konrad, 'because one of the forest snakes
– because, at the very moment that it is about to sink in its
fangs, at that very moment . . . it . . . it has a thing.'

'A thing?' says Dad.

'Yeah, like the other one had when it got into the spaceship.'

'A sudden realisation? Does Ana the half-snake suddenly
realise that she is, in fact, the astronaut Eddi Aldi?'

'No,' says Konrad. He's using the tone of voice that Dad
uses when he explains stuff to Peter, stuff that he really ought

to know already. 'No, that could only have happened if it had touched the crystal. But it suddenly has one of those – those – what d'you call it?'

'A funny feeling?'

'Yes, only not funny.'

'A feeling of security?'

'Something like that.'

'A feeling of confidence?'

'What's that?'

'Well,' says Dad, 'if I trust somebody completely, even though I don't know what he's doing. Just like that. Maybe because I love him. That's having total confidence in the person.'

'Exactly,' says Konrad, exhaling loudly. 'That's exactly what Ana the forest snake has, although she hasn't the faintest idea that she is really Aldi the astronaut.'

'Terrific,' says Dad. 'I'm speechless. So what does she do now?'

'The first thing is that she doesn't bite Deceiver but instead she creeps back to her hide-out in the jungle.'

'Whew! A piece of luck for all concerned.'

'Yes,' says Konrad. And then there's a fairly long pause, during which nobody speaks.

'Well then,' says Dad at last, 'I think the story could certainly go like that. And by the way, was there anything else?'

'Oh, yes,' says Konrad.

It's now or never!

'Could you please drive me, Friederike and a box with a rabbit in it into town tomorrow morning?'

Well, it's out. Whatever happens now, Konrad is already feeling much better.

'Hmm,' says Dad. 'How big is the box?'

'One of those removal packing cases. You know.'

'I do indeed,' says Dad. 'No problem getting a thing like that into the car. Where are you going?'

'You can let us out at Gerhard's toy shop.'

'Right,' says Dad. 'That's on my way.'

So now what? Is the question of questions not going to be asked?

'And what's it all about?' says Dad. 'Why does this rabbit have to be driven into town? So that it gets to see a bit of the big wide world? Or is it its birthday and it's going to be allowed to choose a toy for itself?'

This is the moment to be really strong.

'Dad,' says Konrad, standing up straight and holding his head up. 'Dad, if you had total confidence in me, then you wouldn't ask, you'd just drive us.'

It's very quiet in the living room for a few seconds.

Until Dad says: 'Why should I have such confidence?'

Konrad just shrugs his shoulders. It must look good, the way he's standing there. Pretty cool. Although he's actually shaking from top to toe.

'Oh, I understand,' says Dad. 'Would nine o'clock suit you?'

'That would suit us just fine.'

'So that's settled,' says Dad. 'Get back into bed now quickly, so you get some sleep before your mysterious adventure.'

161

He doesn't have to tell Konrad twice. Mum gets a quick kiss, and Dad a very quick one, and then Konrad runs up the stairs, jumps into bed, wakes up Mattchoo the mouse and tells him what has to be told. Then he falls asleep so quickly that you'd think someone had turned him off like a light.

All Systems Go!

You could easily take it for a normal breakfast, the Bantelmann breakfast on the following morning. Mum is telling them about her latest idea for improving things around the house, Peter almost knocks his chocolate over, and dad is reading something funny out of the paper. It is not, of course, a normal Bantelmann breakfast, but, astoundingly, no one says a word about the most important thing in the world.

Konrad thinks Dad must have forgotten his promise, but at exactly five minutes to nine he stands up and signals to him.

'Let's go,' he says. 'I'll just get the aninal transporter out of the garage. We leave in three minutes.'

Like lightning, Konrad is out and into the hall. Just to be sure, he ties two double knots in his shoelaces. Which is not such a great idea really, because during the course of the day, double-knotted shoelaces get tighter and tighter and start to hurt, and in the evening you can't get them open at all, but it's better to be safe than sorry. Even though it's warm out and doesn't look a bit like rain, Konrad takes his yellow rain jacket with the reflective silver strips off its hook and puts it on. Just in case.

'Have you got money for the bus?' says Mum.

Bus? What bus? Konrad says nothing, but his face must look like a question mark.

'How else were you thinking of getting home?' asks Mum.

'Right,' says Konrad. 'Right. Bus. Money.'

He nods. He does actually have money. He has two ten euro notes and ten euro coins in a little purse and he's put the purse on a string around his neck. It's under his T-shirt and feels rather cold against his chest. He takes it out and shows it to Mum.

'Very professional,' says Mum. 'And do you know our phone number off by heart?'

Konrad says it five times in a row without a mistake.

'Very well,' says Mum. Then she hunkers down on the floor in front of Konrad and puts her hands on his shoulders. 'Promise me you won't do anything silly and that you'll be careful.'

'Yes.' Actually, he's only promising about the being careful part. But Dad has already got the car out, and now is really not the time to be holding a conversation with Mum about not doing anything silly.

Fortunately, Mum accepts his 'yes'. She gives him a kiss, and then he leaves the house and gets into the car. Unfortunately, he has to sit on one of the awful multi-coloured booster seats, because he's still just a kilo too light to sit on a normal seat.

'Seat belt?' asks Dad.

'Yes, it's buckled.'

And then they drive slowly through The Dransfeld.

'Which number exactly?'

'28b.'

Actually, there was no need to tell him the number, because outside Fridz's house, in the middle of the pavement, is the third attempt at rabbit transportation, which – oh joy! – looks exactly like a normal box. On top of the box is a lamp as big as a coffee machine, which is rotating and giving out a harsh red light. When he sees it, Dad laughs loudly, but then he looks in his rear-view mirror and stops laughing.

'I think we are expected,' he says.

Then he stops at the lit-up box and gets out of the car.

Fridz is standing beside the box. She has plaited her hair, and she's wearing a yellow rucksack on her back.

'Hi,' she says and puts out her hand. 'I am Friederike Frenke.'

'Pleasure,' says Dad. He takes her hand. 'I am Konrad Bantelmann's father. Is everything ready for the transportation?'

'Of course,' says Fridz, turning off the rotating lamp. 'I hope this box won't be too heavy for your vehicle.'

'I don't think that will be a problem,' says Dad .

And while Fridz is putting the lamp in front of the door of number 28b, he opens the hatchback and lifts the box into the car. There's a rumbling from inside the box.

'Good heavens!' says Dad. 'What a weight!'

'Yes,' says Fridz. 'It's a so-called prize specimen. Almost ninety-eight kilos when awake. Sleeping, however, seventy-three.'

'Oh. What's he called, the rabbit?'

'He's called The Last of the Flemish Giants Who is All Alone in the Hutch.'

Ouch! thinks Konrad on his booster seat.

But Dad only says, 'A lovely name. Very poetic.'

Then he closes the hatchback, and Fridz sits on Peter's booster seat.

'Hi,' she says.

'Hi.'

'Are we all set?' says Dad.

'We are.'

'Roger. Seat belts all buckled?'

'Buckled.' says Fridz. 'Ready for take-off.'

And off they go.

They're hardly out of The Dransfeld, when Fridz pokes Konrad in the ribs. It hurts. What's wrong with her now? But Konrad clenches his teeth and says nothing.

Fridz says nothing either. Instead, she pokes him again, although not so hard this time, and she pulls a face that means, 'Super!' or maybe, 'Well done!' She's wriggling about on her booster seat, as if someone had scattered itching powder inside her tiger-striped trousers.

So this is what it's like to be praised by Fridz – it's not exactly generous praise; you couldn't call it that. All the same, Konrad thinks maybe it wasn't such a bad idea after all to get involved in this adventure.

Now they're on the road that goes into town. Outside the supermarket, someone is pushing a long row of trolleys across the car park, and at the petrol station, someone is standing on a ladder to change the price of the petrol.

'Look,' says Konrad. 'Is the petrol going up or down in price?'

'What a question!' Fridz taps her forehead to show how wise she is. 'Things only ever get dearer. Nothing ever gets cheaper. Everyone knows that. And so should you.'

Once again, Konrad says nothing. He doesn't look ahead, either, so that he doesn't have to meet Dad's eyes in the rear-view mirror.

Another rumbling comes from the rabbit box.

'Your passenger is getting restless,' says Dad.

'Not to worry. Everything under control.' Fridz pulls a carrot out of her rucksack and holds it up. 'Special carrot. Soaked in Rescue Remedy. Calming and relaxing. I'll give it to him now.'

And she unbuckles her seat belt, turns around to the boot space and somehow manages to stick the carrot into the box. Anyway, a moment later the sound of rabbit teeth on carrot is to be heard.

'Good grief!' says Dad. 'Very professional.'

They drive on for a bit in silence. The traffic is getting heavier and nearly every traffic light is red. Then they get caught behind a bin lorry, with a bin stuck in it. The bin men are banging on the bin with their fists and are shouting so loudly that they can hear it in the car.

'Very unprofessional,' says Fridz, and Dad turns the radio on.

They're nearly there now. Through the big roundabout and they're into Berliner Strasse.

'Next stop, Gerhard's toy shop,' says Dad. 'Passengers with special luggage, stand by!'

'All set,' says Fridz as Dad turns into a parking spot.

'Exit right, please!'

They both get out, and Dad puts the rabbit box on the pavement. 'Good luck, then!' he says and he pats Konrad on the head as he passes him. He has his hand on the car door handle.

Mad! thinks Konrad. Another few seconds and the tricky bit will be over, and Dad actually hasn't asked another thing!

But then Dad lets go of the car door and comes towards him. 'I've just thought of something,' he says.

Right. He has probably thought of asking Fridz who's supposed to be getting this rabbit and why. Konrad feels as if someone has spilt hot cocoa all over his insides. But Dad only pulls his tiny new folding mobile phone out of his pocket and gives it to Konrad.

'Here,' he says. 'You know how to use it. Just in case anything goes wrong, you can ring Mum on this. Okay?'

'Okay,' says Konrad casually, putting the mobile in his pocket.

Dad drives off. He just gives a little wave, and off he goes.

Konrad watches until the blue Passat disappears in the traffic.

'Things are looking bad for you,' says Fridz, who is sitting on the box and rooting about in her rucksack.

'What?'

'Divorce, I mean. Your father is very nice. And being nice is a definite indicator when it comes to divorce. I'd say it's more like three all.'

'You're nuts!' This time it's Konrad who taps his forehead and makes that drilling motion that means the other person is definitely loopy. 'How could being nice mean you are likely to get divorced?'

'Well,' says Fridz. 'If *I* like him, goodness knows who else might feel the same way about him.'

'Like who?'

'Ach, you dumb cluck,' says Fridz, fluttering her eyelashes. 'Other women of course. And if loads of other women think he is nice, then he could very easily go off with one of them.'

'I hate you!' Konrad can't help saying it. It just insisted on being said.

Fridz gets up off the box and puts her rucksack on. 'That's great,' she says. 'Means we'll be together for ages.'

She takes a step towards Konrad and, before he can do a thing about it, he's been kissed by her again. For the third time. This time in the middle of the pavement on Berliner Strasse – and smack on the lips.

Konrad is speechless. People often think they are speechless and they go right on talking, but Konrad really cannot say a word.

'So,' says Fridz. 'Phase one successfully completed. Now for phase two: pulling the wool over the eyes of the victim. Let's go – this is your handle, take it!'

Still speechless, Konrad takes hold of the handle and together they carry the box along Berliner Strasse.

'Are we there yet?' asks Fridz after a few metres, in a silly, childish voice.

'You should know.' Oh! Well, at least the speechlessness has passed.

'I do know. Just there – where it says "Oller's Fashions". That's it. That's where the sneaky snake works.'

Another twenty metres and the pair of them are at the door of the clothes shop.

'What if she sees the box?' asks Konrad.

'She won't. She works on the second floor, and she's far too stupid to be looking out of the window.'

Konrad sits on the box.

'Good luck, so,' he says.

But Fridz doesn't go into the shop. She just looks thoughtfully at the ground. 'Why don't you come with me?' she says at last.

'Why? Are you scared?'

Fridz rolls her eyes. 'Rubbish! It's just that it would look better if you were with me, more convincing. You really can look thick, you know.'

'But what about the box? We can't leave it on the street.'

Now Fridz looks even more thoughtful. 'No, that's right, we can't. Let's just carry it in, and we'll hide it until we're ready to go.'

'Hide it? Where?'

But Fridz has already caught hold of one handle, and Konrad has no choice but to take the other one, and to carry the box into Oller's shop.

Oh my, he thinks.

When they get inside, a shop assistant looks straight at them. But she seems bored, and she looks away again. Two children with a large box – that's nothing to worry about.

'There, at the back,' says Fridz.

She's pointing at a circular clothes stand on which there are women's trousers on special offer, and they're hanging almost down to the floor.

'Is anyone looking?'

No, no one's looking. Fridz parts the trousers with one hand, as if she is opening a curtain, and together they push the box through. The clothes stand looks a bit lopsided now, but Fridz thinks it'll do.

'Ingenious,' she says.

Konrad doesn't agree. There are a few things he'd like to say, but it's all happening so fast. They're up the escalator now to the second floor.

'Men's department,' says Fridz. 'It's typical that this bimbo works in the men's department, isn't it?'

Konrad has no opinion.

In the men's department, a young man is pushing a rack of overcoats along a passageway.

'Ah,' says Fridz. She stands in the middle of the aisle, so that the young man with the coats has to stop. 'Super. Are these the new colours for autumn?' Fridz takes a sleeve and holds it up. 'A deep chocolate brown and a kind of whole-meal grey. Very nice, very smart.'

'Can you let me get by, please, kiddo?' says the young man.

'Of course, kiddo,' says Fridz. 'If you will just tell me

where I can find the senior saleswoman, Fräulein Kristine Ahlberger.'

'Frau Ahlberger is the manageress in the casual and young fashions department,' says the young man. 'Over there, near the lift.'

'Humblest thanks.'

Fridz takes Konrad by the arm. 'Watch this,' she says softly into his ear. 'Look sad and say nothing. Can you manage that much?'

Konrad nods. More skulduggery! And the day is not over yet.

In the casual and young fashions department the new jeans are being piled up on a table. Two men are doing the piling-up, and a woman with very short blonde hair is watching.

Fridz takes Konrad by the hand and goes up to the woman, with Konrad trailing half a pace behind her.

'Hi, Krissi,' says Fridz in a tearful voice.

'Friederike!' says the woman. 'What a surprise! What are you doing here?'

Fridz starts to cry on the spot. Konrad feels his hand getting damp and cold in hers. It must feel like a dead frog. But Fridz doesn't let it go. Instead, she squeezes it hard. And a tear falls from her left eye down her face to her chin.

'Oh, Friederike,' says the woman, 'what's wrong with you?'

The two jeans-pilers look over, and the woman takes Fridz by the shoulder and moves her a bit away from the display table, with Konrad still in tow.

'Tell me, please, what's happened?' asks the woman.

'I –,' says Fridz, 'I –' But she can't get a word out for sobs. Instead, she weeps a second tear, this one out of her right eye.

Man, oh, man! thinks Konrad. What a talent!

And what an effect she is having! The manageress looks quite shocked. She says 'Ach!' and 'Oh dear!' and eventually she hunkers down in front of Fridz, just the way Mum did this morning with Konrad, and strokes her hair. So this is Kristine Crisis. Actually, she seems quite nice. If her hair were just a little bit longer, she could easily be a Dransfeld mother, with a husband and two children of her own and a new house with a front garden, a little beech hedge and a Volkswagen Passat out in front.

Konrad is starting to feel sorry for her. Tomorrow she'll be all lumps and bumps and she'll be scratching the skin off her body with her prettily painted red fingernails. That will not look one bit pretty. She might even cry, and that would make her make-up run. Not a pretty sight either. And all because a certain Konrad Bantelmann put the idea of this rabbit project into the head of a certain Friederike. The poor woman.

But who knows, thinks Konrad. Perhaps she will look so dreadful tomorrow that Fridz's father will leave her and come back to his wife and daughter – and then it would all have been worth it. Then the father could look after his own rabbit, number 28b would finally have a front garden that is just as nice as the other front gardens in The Dransfeld, Fridz's mother wouldn't be unhappy any more and wouldn't have to take any more sleeping pills and Fridz wouldn't be angry and sad any more. That'd be a fine thing! And even if, in exchange for all this, an itchy manageress sat crying her eyes out – well, they'd still have done a good day's work.

Wouldn't they? Yes, of course, thinks Konrad. A good day's work, in spite of everything. You have to harden your heart a bit. No false sympathy.

Out loud, he says, 'All your own fault.'

'Excuse me?' says the woman.

Oh dear, thinks Konrad.

Luckily, Fridz has got her speech back. 'That's right,' she says quickly. 'It's all my own fault. I told her. I said, you are a stupid tramp.'

'Who?' says the woman, looking strange. 'Who's a stupid tramp?'

'Mum.' Fridz acts all worked up. 'And then Mum said, you're a hysterical cow.'

'Who?'

'Me. And then I said, go to hell, I hope you are roasted on a spit and –'

'No, please!' The woman looks as if she wants to clamp Fridz's mouth shut. 'I understand now. You've been fighting with your mum. And what happened then? Did you run away?'

Fridz nods.

'Aha. And who's this with you?'

'Konrad Bantelmann. Number 17a. He's taking care of me. I'm just a woman. Anything could happen to me.' Fridz looks like some little girl in a silly Japanese cartoon. And she's even talking like some silly Japanese cartoon girl. In this silly voice she says: 'Oh, Krissi, I can't go home. Please, please, let me go to your place and wait for Dad. Oh please, that would be so sweet of you.'

Konrad can't bear to look. At least she's let go of his hand so that she can cry on the woman's shoulder.

'Please, please,' she's saying. And on and on: 'Please, please, please.'

Ghastly!

'Of course you can stay at my place.'

'Really?' cries Fridz. 'Really, really? Oh, you're so nice!'

The only thing she didn't do was actually jump for joy. You'd really want to watch yourself with this girl. She should wear a notice around her neck saying, 'BEWARE OF THE WITCH' and 'DANGER! DO NOT COME WITHIN TEN METRES! DO NOT BELIEVE A SINGLE WORD OUT OF THE MOUTH OF THIS PERSON!'

The woman extricates herself, with difficulty, from Fridz's embrace.

'But we'll have to let your mother know, so that she won't be worried.'

'We-ell,' says Fridz slowly.

Konrad pulls Dad's folding mobile out of his pocket and holds it up.

'We told her already,' he says. 'With this.'

He flicks the phone open and shut again. Then he puts it back in his pocket.

'Oh, good,' says the woman. 'Wait till I get you the key.'

She goes to a curtain and disappears behind it.

'How did I do?' asks Fridz softly.

'Disgusting.'

'True. But you were worse.'

'Pst!'

The woman is coming back with the keys. The one with the red top is for the front door, and the blue one is the key to the apartment. Does Friederike know how to get there from here?

'Sure,' says Fridz. 'Stone's throw.'

'Well, then, off you go.'

Fridz has already turned to go, but the woman holds her back.

'I'm very pleased,' she says, 'that you came to me. Maybe we'll get on a bit better from now on.'

'For sure,' says Fridz.

Konrad watches closely. Is she blushing? Even a little? Yes, she's a little bit red.

But by the time they are on the escalator, it's passed.

'Cow,' says Fridz.

Red Trousers

As the two reach the ground floor of Oller's Fashions, Fridz takes Konrad by the arm.

'Watch out,' she says. 'This is the dangerous bit. It's one thing to stick something in some place, but just try getting it back out again, I'm telling you, people watch you like hawks.'

'I get it,' says Konrad.

But as it happens, it's not so much the getting out of the rabbit box that's the problem. The problem is that there where the display unit with the ladies' trousers had been, there's now – nothing!

'Huh?' says Fridz.

Konrad says nothing. This might even be a solution – of sorts.

'Damn,' says Fridz.

'Pst,' says Konrad.

Fridz is now so red in the face that there's hardly any difference between her face and her hair. 'What's happened to the old jackrabbit?' she says.

'Maybe they found him and sent him to the animal shelter.'

'I don't think so.'

'Please,' says Konrad, 'let's get out of here.'

For just a moment he feels quite light-hearted. Maybe Fridz will say, 'Right you are,' and then in ten minutes they could be on the bus and half an hour later they'd be back in The Dransfeld.

'No way!' says Fridz. 'We can't give up now. And anyway, they can't have found the creature.'

'How d'you mean?'

'Just look around you. If these fashion bimbos had found a bunny rabbit, they'd all be standing around the box screeching, "Oh, how sweet," and "Oh, how cute!" *You* know.'

Whereas in actual fact, everything is very quiet in Oller's Fashions.

'We have to find the stand,' says Fridz. 'I bet the box is still stuck in it. Let's go. It's ladies' trousers on special offer that we're after. We'll split up. You go that way, and I'll stick around here.'

And with that, she's off. Konrad wonders briefly if he won't seem suspicious looking for ladies' trousers. But it's probably even more suspicious to stand around in a clothes shop looking stupid – and for this reason, he sets off. As he goes, he's thinking up a few things to say if anyone addresses him.

'I need a nice outfit.'

'I'm looking for a colourful scarf to go with my pale coat.'

'I'm interested in flowery blouses.'

He can come up with any number of sentences like that. Luckily, Konrad has been with Mum often enough in clothes shops. And he's listened to her for hours on end talking to the sales assistants. He'll have no problem thinking of something suitable to say.

As he passes a long row of jackets, he runs his hand along them, which makes the hangers rattle on the rack as if they had something to say. Then he gives a stand of skirts a twirl, and it looks comical, the way the skirts fly up in the air as they ride the merry-go-round.

'Well, young man, what are we looking for?'

'Me?' says Konrad. He turns around to see a shop assistant smiling at him.

'Yes, you.'

'Me? Ah.'

'The children's department is on the third floor.'

'Yes,' says Konrad. Not a very intelligent answer, he knows.

'It's ladies' fashions down here,' says the assistant. 'Or are you looking for something for your mother?'

'Yes,' says Konrad. If only he could think of something else to say!

'And what, exactly?' The sales assistant smiles a tiny bit more.

'Trousers,' says Konrad. 'Ladies' trousers.'

'And where is your mother?'

At home, thinks Konrad. My mother is at home and has no idea what kind of a hoo-ha her hitherto well-behaved son Konrad is creating.

'Back there,' he says and points somewhere or other.

It's all going to come out now.

'In the changing room?'

In the changing room? Yes, why not? Konrad nods a couple of times.

'And now you're looking for the stand with the special offers?'

'Yes!' Konrad is delighted. It's the first time for ages that he's been able to tell the truth.

'You're a great help,' says the assistant. 'Come along. We've just moved the special offers.'

She walks on ahead. Konrad, the great help, follows her.

The stand with the ladies' trousers is now behind a big pillar. Konrad tries to look around him, without moving his head. No sign of Fridz. Maybe she's seen that he's been caught and has gone into hiding.

'Here we are,' says the assistant. 'What size does your mother take?'

'Thirty-six.'

This is one thing Konrad is quite sure of. Mum certainly talks enough about how she's a size thirty-six. She's very proud of it, because size thirty-six means nice and slim. Size thirty-eight means you are disgustingly fat.

'Thirty-six,' says Konrad again. It's lovely to be able to tell the truth twice in a row.

'And what colour is she looking for?' The sales assistant seems a lot friendlier now. She plunges both hands into the ladies' trousers. No, don't do that!

'That pair!' says Konrad quickly. 'Those red ones!'

'That's what I call taste,' says the assistant. 'Strong colours suit slim women very well.'

She pulls the trousers out. Konrad takes them. The sales assistant looks at him. What should he do now? Oh, yes. He must take the red trousers, size thirty-six, to his mother in the changing room. Of course.

'Thank you,' he says.

But his 'Thank you' is of no use. The assistant doesn't go away. *Go away!* thinks Konrad. *Toodle pip! Off you go!*

But thinking doesn't do him any good. She's standing as if rooted to the spot. And she's still looking at him. What else can he do but set off with the red trousers towards the changing rooms?

Konrad goes. Slowly. He can feel the gaze of the sales assistant on his back. He used to think that it only happened in those detective stories of his, where children detected around in abandoned castles, and looks would somehow fall on their backs. But now it seems it really can happen, you actually can feel looks. And not only that. Konrad feels the look propelling him forward. Towards the blinking changing rooms.

There are, in fact, five of them. In three of them, the curtains are open, and in two the curtains are drawn. Eeny, meeny, thinks Konrad, miney, mo. He walks right up, unhesitatingly, to the closed cubicle on the right. The look drilling into his back pushes him onwards. He pulls the curtain aside just a little, and slips inside.

'Hey!' says a woman. She's wearing only her underwear, and she has something in her hand that might be a dress. The woman is fairly young, but Konrad can only guess, because he's looking down and away from the woman.

'Please,' he says softly. 'Please be my mother.' He holds the red trousers up. 'And try these on.'

'Are you mad?' says the woman. 'Or is this some kind of new sales technique?'

'Here, Mum!' says Konrad loud enough for it to be heard outside. 'I've got you a red pair.'

He looks up into the woman's face. She's quite pretty. That makes it easier.

'Please,' he says very softly. 'Please, please! For my sake.'

The woman says nothing for a moment. 'Are you in some kind of trouble?' she asks.

Konrad nods.

'Did you pinch something?'

Konrad shakes his head.

'Well, then, what?'

'I can't explain. Please, be my mother. Just for a minute.'

The young woman laughs, but she puts her hand over her mouth.

'And the trousers,' she says then, 'do I really have to put them on?'

'Yes,' says Konrad. 'But it's a special offer. And I'd say you're definitely a thirty-six.'

'Hey!' says the young woman. 'You know a thing or two.'

She takes the trousers, gets into them, and pulls her short T-shirt over them, showing a bit of stomach.

'What's your name?'

'Konrad.'

'Right, let's get out of here!' The young woman pushes the curtain aside and steps out of the cubicle.

The sales assistant is still outside. She smiles at Konrad. He grins back. The young woman stands in front of a big mirror, puts her hands on her hips and does a twirl.

'What do you think, Konni darling?' she asks. 'Do they suit me?'

She's doing really well. Though *Konni darling* was uncalled for.

'Super, Mumsy!' Konrad calls back.

The assistant smiles again and goes off. Hardly has she disappeared behind a pillar than Fridz appears by a table full of pullovers, flailing her arms like mad.

So she hasn't been caught. Konrad gives a few furtive signals back. He goes over to the young woman at the mirror.

'I'm out of danger now,' he says. 'Thanks a lot for not giving me away.'

'That's okay,' says the young woman. 'Just one question. What do I have to do to get such an amusing son?'

For heaven's sake! Konrad blushes.

'Very well,' says the young woman, patting him on the head. 'You'd better get a move on, agent 007.'

So he does. Fridz is waiting for him by the pullover table.

'I don't believe it,' she says. 'Instead of looking for the bunny, you're making up to a strange woman and disappearing with her into a changing cubicle! And what's this I hear? *Konni darling?* That doesn't sound like you.'

'I –,' says Konrad. He has a lot of explaining to do.

'Oh, you!' says Fridz. 'In the meantime, I've found the

stand. And as I correctly guessed, the box is in it. Come on, Konni darling, you useless creature, at least help me to carry it!'

No, thinks Konrad, don't protest! Don't try to explain anything. That'd only make things worse.

'Anyone watching?' asks Fridz.

'No.'

'Let's do it, then!'

With a bit of pushing and shoving, they get the box out from under the trousers. They take a side each, and start to make their way towards the exit.

The sales assistant from just now is there.

'Well,' she says. 'You're making yourself useful again. Did your mother like the trousers?'

'She's still deciding,' says Konrad.

'And this is your sister?'

'Yes,' says Konrad. 'She's called Friederike. But we call her Fritzi darling'

'That's sweet,' says the assistant.

Ten paces, fifteen paces and they're out on the street again with the box.

'Fritzi darling?' says Fridz. She puts her side of the box down on the pavement. 'That's a bit cheeky of you, my dear!'

Konrad is still holding up his side of the box.

'Can we please get out of here?' he says.

'We can,' says Fridz. 'Anyway, I need my elevenses.'

Fifty metres further on there's a fast-food restaurant, which is already open. The fast-food restaurant belongs to an American company, and it looks exactly like all the other restaurants belonging to this company.

'Here,' says Fridz. 'Here we can have a Thunderburger for once in our lives.'

'Can we take an animal in there?'

'Not if we ask first.'

They go into the fast-food place.

'You stay here with the box,' says Fridz. 'I'll get something for us. It doesn't really matter what, does it?'

That's true. For Konrad Bantelmann is probably the only boy in the whole world who really doesn't like anything you can get in American fast-food restaurants. But he hasn't got time to explain all this, because, in the first place, Fridz has already disappeared in the direction of the counter, and secondly, there are three bigger boys standing there. These bigger boys are wearing jackets on which a lot of words are printed, the most up-to-date sports shoes on their feet and very trendy haircuts on their heads. Basically, not a problem. To everyone his taste, Dad always says. The only thing is that the biggest of the bigger boys is pointing at the box with an outstretched arm.

'Hey,' he says. 'Whassat?'

If only it wasn't the school holidays! thinks Konrad. Otherwise, this trio would be stuck in some classroom, copying numbers off the board, or doing something else useful, instead of hanging around in this particular fast-food restaurant, taking an interest in other people's boxes.

'Whassat, huh?'

By now, Fridz is at the counter, and it's too far to call out to her.

Maybe I'll give the truth a whirl again, thinks Konrad.

It worked once today already.

'A Flemish Giant,' he says.

'Huh?'

'It's an extraordinarily enormous rabbit. Could weigh up to seven kilos.'

'Cool! Gi's a look!'

No, the truth is not working. The three bigger boys are already kneeling around the box and their six hands are tearing at the lid.

'Careful, it bites,' says Konrad

'Ha ha!'

'It has an infectious disease.'

'Yuck!'

Lying isn't working either. The lid is off now, and six hands are groping down into the box.

'Hey, is he fat or what? Man!'

The ears of the giant rabbit appear over the edge of the box.

'Please!' says Konrad. 'Please, leave him in the box.'

'Don't make such a fuss!' says the biggest of the bigger boys. 'Give it to me. I want it.'

And he gets it.

'Wow!' he says, falling back on his bottom. 'What a giant! Let's take him into the kitchen and have him roasted.'

The other two are hollering with delight.

Konrad clutches his chest, where his purse is hanging. Maybe he could offer them a ransom. But he doesn't get that far.

'Ow!' shouts the biggest boy, letting the rabbit go. 'It bit me.'

He's holding his finger up, and it does look as if it has been nibbled a bit.

Bravo, thinks Konrad. The gigantic rabbit really has bitten him. The truth is giving him a run for his money today.

And he has something else to be pleased about. Because now the Belgian devil is running up the aisle between the tables towards the counter. This does not go unnoticed.

'Eeeeek!' someone shouts. 'A mouse. A gigantic, horrible mouse!'

'Help!' shouts someone else. 'Help!'

'Waaah,' shrieks a girl. 'It's revolting! They put rabbits in the burgers.'

This makes another couple of girls laugh so hard that they almost choke.

Konrad runs after the rabbit. He bangs into a table, a paper cup falls over and someone yells, 'No, my new trousers!'

I've nearly caught him, thinks Konrad, but just then the rabbit twists away from him and disappears under the tables. Unfortunately, Konrad can't brake that quickly. He has to take one more step, which brings him smack up against Fridz, who is just coming away from the counter with a tray.

'Have you flipped?' says Fridz.

This is not the moment for a discussion like this.

'A rat!' yells someone. 'I saw a rat!'

Anyone who hasn't already been yelling starts to do so now. Konrad is on the floor. As he is crawling under the tables, a chair falls over and almost gets him on the head.

'Konrad!' That's Fridz.

No time! The rabbit is turning left, and Konrad is after him, on all fours. Someone comes towards him. The rabbit turns right and now it's in the aisle again. Konrad is right behind him.

For a moment, the rabbit stops, and then it runs towards the exit. Its back legs are stretched right out and its little white tail is waving in the air.

'It's getting away! Oh no, it's getting away!'

Konrad has never heard Fridz sounding like this. He can't see her, but she sounds dreadful. The rabbit is now about three metres from the door. Luckily, it's closed. Oh no, it's not, not any more! The biggest of the bigger boys, the one whose finger was bitten, pulls it wide open.

'Out with the beast!' he shouts. 'It bit me! It's rabid!'

The screeching in the fast-food restaurant gets even louder, if that is possible. Oh, no!

Konrad is on his feet again. He's running. More precisely, he's getting up speed. And then he jumps. He jumps like a footballer when they've just scored a goal and really want to celebrate it. He leaps horizontally, lands on his stomach, and slides, with outstretched arms, right across the polished floor of the fast-food restaurant.

'Yes!' yells someone. 'Catch it!'

It's Fridz.

And Konrad catches it. At the very last moment, just as it is about to get away, his right hand grabs the right back leg of the rabbit. And he holds on for dear life. The rabbit struggles and kicks, its claws scrabbling on the floor, and it's making this pitiful squeaking noise. But Konrad holds on tight. There he is, flat out on the floor, with one hand on the rabbit, and all around him is yelling and roaring and din.

'Police!' shouts someone. 'Police, fire brigade, police!'

Great idea!

Then Fridz is beside him. She gets hold of the rabbit with both hands and presses it to her.

'Scram!' she says. 'Let's make ourselves scarce.'

And she's out the door like a shot. Konrad struggles to his feet. Hands are reaching for him, but he shakes them off. He just wants to get out of here.

Out on the street, he looks around.

'Wait!' he calls, but Fridz is not waiting. She's running, with a pair of rabbit ears wiggling in the air over her shoulder.

Konrad has a job not to lose sight of her as he runs to catch up with her. She takes a left into a side street, and then a right. Konrad can hardly breathe and he's starting to get a stitch in his right side as Fridz runs into a courtyard and finally stops in front of a building.

'Here, take it!' she says, as Konrad catches up with her, shoving the rabbit into his arms. And then she's off again, dragging him after her into the house.

Konrad follows her in. What's all this? He looks around: a staircase, a door down into the cellar, a few postboxes on the wall. And no one to be seen.

Oof! He sits down on the bottom step of the stairs.

'I'm all in,' he says. 'Finished.'

The rabbit in his arms has gone totally still. It's just shaking a bit.

'I'm finished,' he says again.

Secret Weapon

'Okay,' says Fridz. 'Take a deep breath. Then we're off again.'

She sits down beside Konrad on the stairs. She's pretty out of breath too.

Konrad takes a few deep breaths. Not so that he can go on in a moment, but because he has something difficult to say. Something very difficult.

'I'm finished,' he says. 'I can't go on, and I don't want to go on. I'm not playing this game any more.'

He takes another breath. 'I'm not doing this rabbit thing with you any more.'

'Fine,' says Fridz. 'I understand. It was just a bit much for you.'

Konrad says nothing. He knows that he's the one who saved the whole situation, and it's enough for him that he knows it. He doesn't have to say it. No, he doesn't have to. He only needs to look straight ahead and put on a particular kind of face.

'Oh, very well,' says Fridz. She's seen the face. 'You were the great hero. The world champion Flemish Giant catcher. But now we're going up to distribute bunny hairs, right?'

'Wrong,' says Konrad.

'And why not, if you please?' Fridz is back on her feet.

She is standing in front of Konrad, looking down on him.

'Because it's wrong.'

'You don't say.'

'Yes, what we're doing is mean.'

'True.' Fridz takes off her rucksack, sits it down in front of her and takes a look inside. 'It's totally mean, what we're doing. I'm terribly sorry about that. But unfortunately, it has to be done.' She takes a carrot out of the rucksack. 'And anyway, it was your idea.'

'I –,' says Konrad.

'Please!' Fridz taps Konrad on the head with the carrot. 'Let's not talk about it now. It can happen that a person gets the jitters just as things are about to come to a head. No problem. Give me the bunny and I'll go on up and do the rest myself.'

'No,' says Konrad.

'What?' Fridz lets the carrot fall. She hunkers down and puts her head forward until it touches Konrad's head. 'What did you say?'

'I'm not doing it any more – and neither is Paul.'

'Are you nuts? Who is Paul?'

'This is Paul.' Konrad strokes the rabbit's head.

'Since when?'

'Always. He's just told me. And he's also told me that he doesn't want to make anyone come out in a rash.'

'You're driving me crazy! Give me the creature!'

Fridz hurls the carrot into a corner behind her. Then she makes to take the rabbit out of Konrad's arms. But Konrad looks at her, she looks at him, and then she drops her arms. For a while, the two of them squat there looking at each other, head to head, saying nothing.

'Now, listen,' says Fridz at last. 'It's my rabbit. You just hand it over, and then, as far as I am concerned, you can vamoose. Is that clear?'

'The rabbit belongs to your father.'

Fridz stands up. 'Rubbish!' she says loudly. Very loudly. 'He doesn't take care of it. He doesn't care about anything. Not about his rabbit, not about my mum and not about me. He only cares about his harebrained Kristine.' She almost shouts the last sentence. 'And that is why I am going to take the bunny rabbit, and go up to the apartment with it and rub everything all over with it, just as we planned. Do you hear me?'

She grabs Konrad by the shoulders and shakes him so hard that he has trouble holding onto Paul.

'As we planned,' says Fridz again.

Then she starts crying. And this time it's for real. There isn't the slightest doubt about that.

'Come on!' wails Fridz. 'You've got to help me. You promised.' She slips down beside him on the bottom step and wails, her head on her arms.

Somewhere, a door opens and steps are to be heard on the stairs.

'Let's go somewhere else,' says Konrad.

Fridz doesn't seem to hear him. She's still crying, only a little more quietly.

'You promised,' she says. 'You promised.'

The steps are getting close. A woman is coming down

the stairs with a small child in her arms.

'Could I get past?' she says.

Fridz doesn't look up. Konrad moves aside a little.

'Aw!' says the woman. 'What have you got there? Is it a hare?' The child in her arms squeals and stretches out its arms. 'And what are you doing here anyway? Who are you going to see?'

'We're just leaving,' says Konrad.

He is trying to get Fridz up off the floor, but with the rabbit in his arms, it's not all that easy.

'Hey!' says the woman. 'You haven't answered my question.'

Konrad knows this. But this is not quite the moment for telling the truth. He gets Fridz onto her feet at last and pushes her towards the door.

'And why is your sister crying?' asks the woman.

She always gets sad when people ask her questions. Konrad thinks it, but he doesn't say it. Instead, he opens the door with his elbow, and nudges Fridz through it with his shoulder.

'Come on,' he says.

The rabbit is starting to slip out of his grasp. He pushes it up as high as he can on his chest and walks on, with Fridz bringing up the rear. Slowly, step by step, but surely. She's still crying a bit, just a little bit.

They cross the yard and out onto the street, then left, and left again. All the time, Konrad is thinking. Although you couldn't really call it thinking. At least not if by thinking you mean something orderly. Konrad is not thinking in an orderly way. More than a dozen thoughts are lumbering around in his head, just like the rabbit when he was in the hutch. They are going around in circles, here, there and everywhere and if Konrad tries to get hold of one of them, it slips between his fingers and is gone. Moreover, all the thoughts are difficult, much more difficult than carrying Paul, the Flemish Giant. And he's pretty heavy! So heavy that Konrad isn't going to be able to carry him for much longer.

Which way are they going anyway? Across Berliner Strasse and back to the roundabout. Yes, there's the little park. Could he make it that far? No, definitely not. Paul weighs a ton.

Konrad turns around. Fridz is still behind him. She's looking at her feet, and she's sniffling. She has her rucksack in her hand, trailing it almost on the ground.

'Wait a minute,' says Konrad. He stops so that Fridz almost bumps into him. 'There's something I want to try.'

Konrad signals to her to put the rucksack down and open it. She does as he wants and Konrad tries to get the rabbit into the rucksack. It works. Most of Paul fits; only his head is sticking out of the top, which is good, because of breathing.

Konrad takes the rucksack on his shoulders. It's still heavy, but it's easier. They walk on, Konrad in front, Fridz coming silently behind him.

At the big roundabout, they have to cross the road three times, and at last they're in the little park. Konrad takes the rucksack off and sits on the first bench. Fridz sits down beside him, and the two of them sit there silently for a full quarter of an hour, during which the rabbit thoughts are running riot in Konrad's head.

After a quarter of an hour, the thoughts have finally settled down into the corners of his brain. Now maybe he can get hold of them.

'Fridz,' says Konrad.

'Hmm.'

'I have something to tell you. Are you listening?'

'Hmm.'

'Well,' says Konrad. 'Pay attention now. In a forest, a jungle actually, a long way from here, a long time ago now, a spaceship from the planet Klimbambium landed. But it was damaged by the impact of the landing; so badly damaged that it can't be started again.'

After quite a long time, Fridz looks at Konrad.

'Huh?' she says.

Good, thinks Konrad. Press on.

'Exactly,' he says. 'And the two extraterrestrial astronauts morphed into a double forest snake, in order to guard the spaceship. Because under no circumstances must extraterrestrial spaceships be discovered by humans, because chaos would ensue. As we know.'

'Tell me, are you out of your tree?' Fridz's eyes are still puffy from crying, but she is starting to look a bit better.

'No,' says Konrad quickly. 'The problem is just that the double forest snake didn't notice another extraterrestrial in human form arriving on earth in order to prevent the scientist Franzkarl Findouter from taking the spaceship out of the jungle and into a laboratory.

'It's getting worse,' says Fridz. 'That is the stupidest story I have ever heard.'

If Dad could hear this, thinks Konrad.

'I'm not finished yet,' he says. 'You'll find the next bit interesting, for sure. The scientist Franzkarl Findouter, who is dead set on winning the Nobble Prize, he has recently left his family and now he's living with his assistant, Dr Kristine Crisis.'

'You've flipped,' says Fridz. 'It's all been too much for you. Could I have the phone for a sec? I'd like to ring the loony bin.'

Konrad puts a hand on his pocket.

'But,' says Fridz, 'you don't need to be afraid. A couple of nice men will come with stout ropes and take you into a lovely room with lots of nice soft foam on the walls. You can converse all day long there with forest snakes.'

'Very funny,' says Konrad. 'Perhaps we could work that into the story later, but not right now. Now we're at the chapter where Franzkarl Findouter's only daughter Luise is taking revenge on her father's new girlfriend.'

'Ah!' says Fridz.

'Yeah. She is desperately angry with this Kristine. She wants to do something very mean to her. Guess what she does?'

'Ho ho.' Fridz taps her finger on her forehead. 'Don't tell me she lets a rabbit into her flat so that she gets an allergic reaction?'

'Wrong,' says Konrad.

'Wrong?'

'Yes, quite wrong.' He takes the rucksack onto his lap. By now, Paul has got both front paws out and they're peeping out of the top of the rucksack, which looks quite comical.

'The Kristine in the story hasn't got an allergy to fur. So this Luise has to do something else.'

'What, then?' says Fridz.

'Something much worse, but I can't say any more.'

'Much worse? Great. She sets her flat on fire?'

'That's stupid. Anyone can do that. It has to be something smart. You see, this Luise is actually pretty smart. I would go so far as to say very smart indeed. I think she's the smartest girl there ever was.' Konrad gives a wink.

'Hmm,' says Fridz, wriggling around on the park bench. 'What worse thing does she do, what smarter thing? I can't guess. Why don't you tell me?'

Good question. The right answer would be, 'Because I don't know myself.' And because you must guess it. But today is a day on which we just don't know when it's better to tell the truth and when not.

'You'll think of something,' says Konrad. 'You're just as smart as this Luise.'

'Wait.' Fridz is getting even more anxious. Paul looks at her out of his rucksack and takes his left paw back in. Just to be on the safe side, perhaps.

'I know!' cries Fridz. 'She ties this Kristine to a tree, sprinkles salt on her feet and gets a goat to lick the salt off.'

'That's mean,' says Konrad. 'But is it smart?'

'No,' says Fridz.

'Try again, then.'

'Right. She orders her twenty-five pizzas every evening with lots and lots of garlic on them. Is that smart?'

Konrad shakes his head.

'You're driving me mad. What is smart, please?'

'If you don't know,' says Konrad, 'how could anyone know?'

Fridz sits very still again. A few big boys come by, stop and point at Paul in the rucksack. One of them says something. Something that big boys always say before they come over and start making trouble.

'Get lost!' says Konrad. 'Or I'll call the police.' He takes the mobile out of his pocket and flicks it open.

It works. The big boys walk on.

Fridz is still sitting quietly. She didn't notice a thing. She must be thinking. What is especially mean and at the same time, especially smart? What?

'I've got it!' she cries out loud. A few more people turn around and Paul draws his left paw back into the rucksack as well.

'Tell me!'

'Luise goes to this Kristine – the one in the story – and says to her that she doesn't like her and that she's a stupid floozy.'

'Hmm,' says Konrad. 'Maybe that's mean. But what makes it smart?'

'Oho!' says Fridz. She shifts over to Konrad and the tip of her nose is once again a millimeter from his. 'Because it's true,' she says very softly. 'And it's smart to tell the truth.

You can always tell people the truth and they can't hold it against you. You can't be punished for it either.' Fridz stands up. 'Let's go,' she says. 'That's what we'll do now.'

'What?'

'Well, what do you think? Stick Paul on your back, and we'll be off.'

What could he say to that? The best thing would be to say nothing at all. And so Fridz and Konrad go back across the three streets at the roundabout. Only this time, Fridz is in front and Konrad is trailing along behind with Paul on his back. When people see Paul, they have a laugh and pass remarks.

The sales staff in Oller's Fashions pass remarks too. For example, that they haven't got anything in that size.

'Ha ha,' says Fridz as she goes by. Very witty. Maybe they could show her the way to the fur department. She's got fresh supplies. So fresh, it's still warm.

'You're a character,' say the sales assistants.

On the second floor, it's pullovers that are being piled up this time.

The manageress, Frau Kristine Ahlberger, is in the middle of the passageway, and she turns round just as Konrad and Fridz step off the escalator.

'Friederike!' she says. 'Could you not get the door open?' She's about to come towards them.

'Stop!' cries Fridz. 'Not a step further!'

'What's up?'

'Ten steps back!' says Fridz. 'We are in possession of a dreadful secret weapon and we're not afraid to use it!'

She makes a sign to Konrad. He turns around and shows Paul in the rucksack.

'Just stay where you are! Otherwise you'll get deadly fur itch.' Fridz has to say it loudly, because the manageress has already turned on her heel and is at least two trouser racks away.

'But, Friederike,' she says from there.

'The key is fine,' says Fridz across the department. 'And by the way, you can have it back.' She drops the keyring onto the floor and gives it a kick so that it clinks across the passage. A few customers are standing around watching and more are appearing from other departments.

'I've come to say something to you,' cries Fridz. 'I want to tell you I think you're stupid. And mean. You've taken away my dad. You mean, stupid cow. If I could have a wish come true, I'd wish you on the moon. I don't like you, and that is never, ever going to change, no matter how nice you are to me.'

'But,' says the woman. She has quite an audience now and she looks like someone who doesn't know what to do. She takes a step forward.

'Don't move!' says Fridz. 'Remember the fur here. And think about your own hide. We wouldn't like anything to happen to you.'

The manageress stays where she is. Even more people have popped up out of nowhere to see what's going on. Droves of people are pouring into the casual and young fashions department.

'Is there a problem, Frau Ahlberger?' asks a strong, masculine voice. 'Or can you manage?'

'No, no, everything's fine.'

Konrad has never been so aware that someone is lying. Nothing is fine. Nobody is able to manage anything here. And everyone in the casual and young fashions department can see that.

'Friederike,' says the manageress. 'You're a big girl now. It's time you understood. Your dad and I, we –'

'Rubbish,' cries Fridz. 'I'm not big. I'm actually small for my age. One metre forty-two. And I'm also a bit silly. I don't have to understand anything. I think you are both just mean, and that's that. And just so you know, from now on I'll have Konrad here with me all the time. And Paul. Just remember that if you want to come sidling up to me. Understand?'

Fridz gets Konrad to show off the rabbit again, and then she signals to him that it's time to go. Konrad is very quick to agree to that.

'Goodbloodybye!' cries Fridz.

And they wriggle their way, with great difficulty, through all the people. There might be as many as one hundred of them.

'Watch it,' says Fridz. 'People with animal allergies, please stand back.'

It might even be two hundred. Konrad can't be sure.

'Frau Ahlberger,' says the strong, masculine voice from somewhere. 'Please come into my office.'

They can hear it from the escalator.

Goodbye, Paul!

I'm hungry now,' says Konrad. 'And so is Paul.'

The three of them are back on the little bench in the park. None of them has said anything so far, so Fridz is a little taken aback by this.

'Hey!' she says. 'What did you say?'

'That we're hungry, me and Paul.'

'Hmm,' says Fridz. She's obviously thinking about something else.

Konrad tries again. It's not often that he's really hungry. When it happens, it's a good idea to take advantage of it. And he has money with him, and no parents to tell him what he should eat.

'Over there,' he says, 'there's a café there where they do just pancakes. Pancakes with sugar, pancakes with jam, pancakes with –'

'– with trouble,' says Fridz. 'Have you no notion what's going on?'

'Sure I have,' says Konrad. 'We'll have a pancake, maybe two and then we'll take the bus home.' He thinks a bit more. 'We'll just have to get Paul to stick his head down a bit in the rucksack.'

Fridz rolls her eyes. 'Man!' she says out loud. 'Don't you understand? Kristine is sure to be ringing my dad and then he'll call my mum.'

Konrad doesn't know what this has to do with pancakes. He can't really think properly about it, because ever since he uttered the word 'pancake', his hunger has been getting worse by the second.

'Man!' says Fridz again. 'Do you really not understand? They'll be after us.'

Konrad swallows. 'How d'you mean?'

'How do I mean? How do I mean?' Fridz leaps up. 'I mean that they'll be all over the place looking for us. Maybe they've told the police already.'

'But why? We didn't do anything.'

Fridz looks at Konrad and puts her head on one side.

'Well . . .' says Konrad. Maybe they've done a little something. Maybe even more than a little.

'You see!' Either Fridz is a mindreader, or what Konrad is thinking is written all over his face. 'And that's why they're going to be looking for us, they're going to find us, and they are going to punish us,' says Fridz. 'I'll probably be sent to a children's home for life, where I'll only have a sack of straw to sleep on and I'll have to do cross-stitch all day long.'

Oops! thinks Konrad. That's an awful thought. On the other hand, Fridz seems to be having a great time imagining such terrible things.

'I think,' he says slowly, 'I think people who tell the truth don't get punished.'

'Well, it's not exactly a punishment,' says Fridz. 'It's revenge. Mean, bloody revenge! That's how parents are. And parents don't care about the law.'

'Hmm,' says Konrad. 'And what'll happen to me?'

'You?' Fridz frowns. 'They'll make you become a keeper in the petting zoo.'

Konrad laughs.

'But Paul will come off worse. He'll end up in the oven. They'll make rabbit sweet-and-sour out of him. And as an extra punishment, you and I will have to eat him up, all by ourselves.'

'You're nuts,' says Konrad.

'I'm nuts?' says Fridz. 'Fair enough. But what about you? Do you really think we're going to have a jolly bus ride home, and they'll all say, "Hello!", nice and cheery, and then everything will go on as before?'

Actually, Konrad would prefer if his parents never heard a single word about what happened today.

'Here they come!' Fridz points towards the roundabout, where there is, in fact, a police car.

Konrad looks at it and says nothing. The police car drives once around the roundabout and then it turns into Berliner Strasse. A few seconds pass, and then the mobile in Konrad's trouser pocket rings.

'Don't answer!' says Fridz. 'It's a trap.'

But Konrad can't help it. He has to open the mobile and press the green key.

'Hello?' he says carefully into the mouthpiece.

It's Dad, wondering where they are.

'In the little park by the roundabout.'

And have they delivered the rabbit?

'Yeah, sure.' Lie! Or is it?

And otherwise everything's okay?

'Yes. Fine.' Which it is, isn't it?

So when will they be home?

'Soon.'

Silence.

'Well, bye then, Dad.' Konrad presses the button, folds the mobile and sticks it in his pocket.

'Congratulations,' says Fridz. 'A stroke of genius. Well done. Now they know exactly where we are. There's no point in trying to run away now.'

She leans back and stretches out her legs.

'Sorry,' says Konrad.

'Doesn't matter. We wouldn't have got very far anyway. Besides, I really don't feel like running away. I still want to eat. Where's this pancake shop of yours?'

'Over there,' says Konrad. And to keep the conversation off the topic of the police, he hoists the rucksack up on his shoulders.

'You go first,' says Fridz.

She pulls a carrot out of her pocket and as they're walking along, she lets Paul nibble at it. He's delighted. At least, he keeps kicking Konrad hard in the back with his hind paws, every time he takes a bite of the carrot. Konrad finally understands why Dad moans so much when he's telling bedtime stories.

Just as the three of them reach the pancake café, a man in a white apron is opening the door.

'Hello, you two,' he says. 'Hungry already?'

'Hello, you one,' says Fridz. 'I have a question for you

too. May we take a rabbit in, if we promise that it will stay nicely in its rucksack?'

Hey! thinks Konrad. Telling the truth is getting fashionable. It looks like it's going to be the hit of the season.

'Okay,' says the man in the apron. Then he says, 'Wow!' He points at Paul. 'That's a Flemish Giant.'

'Bull's-eye,' says Fridz. 'A hundred marks.'

'How come you're carrying him around? Is that the only outing he gets?'

'Not at all,' says Fridz. 'We just wanted to show him the big wide world.'

Come off it, thinks Konrad. She really has a nerve. But she is funny.

The man in the apron would like to get a closer look at Paul. Would he be allowed out of the rucksack?

'Oh,' says Fridz. They've had bad experiences with that.

'Come on in, so.' Apron man leads them into the café and then through a long passageway out to a small yard where there are tables and benches. Konrad takes the rucksack off and Fridz takes Paul out very carefully. She holds him by the fur on his back, so that he can't get away.

'Here you go. This is Paul.'

'Good grief!' says the man with the apron. He takes Paul, presses him in various places, turns his head and his ears and all the time he's looking pretty excited.

'That's a wonderful specimen!' he says.

'Correct,' says Fridz. 'That's what it says on his pedigree. By the way, are you the cook here?'

'Of course I'm the cook.'

'Help!' says Fridz. 'This fellow wants to cook Paul.'

She pokes Konrad in the side. 'I told you. The revenge is starting.'

The cook laughs. 'Nonsense!' he says. 'I only make pancakes. I have Flemish Giants at home, but I haven't often seen one as fine as this lad here.'

He feels Paul's fur again. Paul keeps still. 'Has he ever won anything?' asks the cook.

'Sure. Medals,' says Fridz. 'And a cup. Silver.' Then she wrinkles her nose.

Konrad knows the signs. She's thinking about something.

'He's for sale,' she says.

'I beg your pardon?' says Konrad.

'Oh, really?' says the cook. He widens his eyes and feels Paul all over.

'Can he,' he says, 'ah . . . I mean . . . can he . . . have baby rabbits?'

'No,' says Fridz. 'He can't, because he's a boy. But he could make some with a doe. He's done it before.'

'Doe?' asks Konrad.

'Girl rabbit,' says Fridz, 'that's what you call them.'

The cook is all wound up. Would they really be allowed to sell Paul? They're only children!

'You can phone my father,' says Fridz. 'He won't mind.'

She makes a sign to Konrad, and he shows off his mobile phone.

'How much?'

Konrad watches Fridz's face. She clearly hasn't got a clue what a Flemish Giant costs. And neither has he.

'I'll make a suggestion,' says the cook. 'I bet you like pancakes, do you?'

Konrad nods so hard that you can hear him doing it.

'Well, then, I'll give you a voucher in exchange for the rabbit, which will allow you to come and have pancakes once a week.'

Fridz squeezes up her eyes. 'For how long?'

'Two months?'

'Hmm,' says Fridz. 'Three.'

'Agreed.'

'And if you get a medal for him or a cup, then another month. And if he has children, then for every child, another week.'

The cook laughs. He agrees. 'But only for you and your brother.'

'Ah,' says Konrad.

Fridz gives him a kick in the ankle.

'Okay,' she says. 'Only for me and my brother. But we need to have it in writing.'

The cook puts Paul in a box, in which there used to be fruit, and he puts two boards over it so that he can't get out.

'No problem,' he says. 'I'll have him sent home to my house. Then he'll have company. And I'll make you two giant pancakes with everything.'

'But first, you have to wash your hands' says Fridz. 'Anyone who's been handling an animal must wash his hands before eating or cooking.'

'Boy,' says the cook, 'you're a character.'

He shakes his head, lifts both hands up in the air and goes into the café.

'But properly, and with soap!' cries Fridz after him. Then she squats down by the fruit box and pushes one of the boards aside a little.

Konrad squats down beside her. Fridz strokes Paul's head.

'Well, you,' she says, 'we've sold you.'

'Are you sad?'

Fridz nods. Then the two of them say nothing for a while. They just sit by the box and scratch Paul behind the ears, one on either side.

'Well, then,' says Fridz at last. 'So long, Paul.'

She stands up and pulls Konrad by the ear.

'Come on, bro! Now to fill our bellies. Let's see how many pancakes will fit into Friederike Frenke.'

The table has been laid for them in the cafe. The cook has even put a candle on the table and lit it. Fridz gives a little squeal of delight. Beside the candle lies the voucher for the free food, and on each of the two giant pancakes that are spilling over the edges of the plates, the cook has drawn a rabbit with sugar, honey, chocolate and jam. They are clearly Flemish Giants. You can tell because they are so big.

Just an hour later, Fridz and Konrad are out on the street in front of the café. Fridz is holding her stomach. 'Phew,' she says. 'It's great that we don't have to carry Paul any more. What'll we do now?'

The phone in Konrad's pocket rings again.

'Say we're not at home,' says Fridz.

This time it's Mum. Konrad can tell from her voice that something has happened.

Where is he?

Konrad answers.

And is Friederike with him?

Yes, she is.

'Listen, Konrad,' says Mum. 'Friederike's mother is standing here beside me. Can you put Friederike on, please?'

'Just a moment,' says Konrad. He presses the mute button.

'Your mum, for you.'

Fridz shakes her head.

'What'll I say?'

'Dunno.'

Mute button off.

'Mum,' says Konrad into the mobile. 'Fridz doesn't want to talk.'

There's talk going on at the other end of the line, at home in the Bantelmanns' house. Konrad can't catch it all, but he understands what it's about. Frau Frenke is worried, and she wants Fridz to come home right away. Right away as in immediately.

That's what Mum says into the phone, and Konrad says it to Fridz, after he's pressed the mute button.

But Fridz shakes her head again. 'I want to do something nice first.'

Mute button off.

'Mum,' says Konrad. 'We have something else to see to.

We'll be home in two hours.' He tries to say it in such a way that no mother in the world would be the least bit worried about it. He says it in his deepest voice, the way Dad does when Peter has tummy ache and is afraid he is going to have to have an operation.

'I'd prefer if you came now,' says Mum. 'Should I come and pick you up?'

As far as Konrad is concerned, that'd be fine. But Fridz just stands there on the kerb, trying to kick a little stone onto the roadway, such a tiny stone that she can't get it with the toe of her shoe at all.

'No,' says Konrad. 'We'll be home in two hours, for sure. Bye, Mum.'

He presses the 'hang up' button. How do you turn the thing off altogether? Maybe it's the little button with the X on it? The screen goes blank and Konrad folds the mobile over.

In the meantime, Fridz has finally managed to get the stone. It bounces off a tyre and ricochets back onto her shin.

'Ouch!' she says.

'Come on,' says Konrad. 'We have two hours to do something nice.'

He thinks for a few seconds. Should he or shouldn't he? What does he mean, should he? It has to be done.

So he comes out with it, 'Two hours and thirty euro.'

'Thirty euro?'

Konrad tugs on the string around his neck until the little purse peeks out from under his T-shirt.

'Did you break your piggy-bank?'

'Yeah, well,' says Konrad.

'And you can lend me some?'

'Sure!'

'Well, then, let's go!' says Fridz.

They set off towards the pedestrian area of town, where the big department stores are.

Fridz takes Konrad's hand. At first, he doesn't even notice. And when he does notice, he also notices that he doesn't mind a bit.

Back in The Dransfeld

It's only a few metres from the bus stop on the main road to the entrance to Hedwig Dransfeld Strasse. Thirty metres, Konrad would say, if he wasn't so bad at guessing this kind of thing. In any case, it's a long thirty metres, because Fridz is getting slower with every step. If she keeps this up, Konrad thinks, she'll soon come to a halt altogether. And that's exactly what she does, just at the entrance to The Dransfeld.

'Do I have to go in?' she asks.

'Yes, you have to.'

'Will you come with me?'

Konrad taps his forehead. What a question! Where else would he be going?

So they walk into Hedwig Dransfeld Strasse. On the left are numbers 2a and 2b, on the right, numbers 1a and 1b. As always.

The beech hedges are still there, and it's hard to say if they've grown a bit in the meanwhile. A couple of Passats and a few other hatchbacks are parked at the kerb or in the driveways. If it were dark, then the china geese in the kitchen windows would certainly be lit up.

'Do you like living here?' asks Fridz.

'Depends.'

'On what?'

Now they're as far as 5a and 5b.

'Depends who else lives here.'

'Oh, yeah,' says Fridz. 'You know loads of people, don't you?'

Konrad thinks about his list and about what happened the other day in the supermarket, the way they made fools of themselves in front of everyone.

'Hmm,' he says. He wouldn't like to say anything more on this point.

'I know hardly anyone,' says Fridz. 'Apart from you.'

Number 9a and 9b. And now they're at the bend in Hedwig Dransfeld Strasse.

'Wrong,' says Fridz. 'I know my mum. As it happens, she lives here too. In the same house, even; imagine! And I met your dad too, recently. But that's about it. My dad doesn't live here.'

'Oh?' says Konrad, as if he hadn't known that at all.

'Oh, yes,' says Fridz. 'Did you know, my dad is actually a researcher. Something to do with snakes. Or missiles. In any case, he can't be at home, because he's always in some jungle or other.'

'That's very interesting.'

'Oh, yeah.' Fridz has taken her rucksack off and now she's dangling it on her arm. 'My dad lives a very exciting life. And he brings me home the craziest things. Really exceptional presents. Recently, he actually brought me a real live Kristine. One starting with a K. From a long way off. But I didn't want her. You know, I just didn't have the space for her, and anyway, all my pocket money would have to go on food for her. No, thank you, I said. Not for me. You can take her off and set her free in the woods.'

Konrad wanted to laugh, but he didn't.

Number 11a. From here, you can see more than half of The Dransfeld. Konrad and Fridz walk more slowly.

A few houses further on, people are standing on the street.

'Would you look at that,' says Fridz.

There are five of them. Four big ones and a little one. Konrad doesn't know one of the men, but the others are Fridz's mother and his own family. Fridz waves at them.

'Coo-ee!' she cries. 'Coo-ee. Here we are!'

'You're silly,' says Konrad.

'I'm not silly. I'm afraid.'

The five people take a step towards them, as far as the driveway of number 15b. Fridz's mother puts her arms around Fridz and hugs her close. Then she kisses her on the forehead, and her red hair falls forward on top of Fridz's. Konrad's dad tweaks Konrad by the ear, and Mum squats down in front of him and takes him in her arms.

Peter steps on his toes, accidentally, of course. 'By the way,' he says. That's all: by the way.

Otherwise, no one speaks for a few seconds. Maybe thirty seconds, Konrad guesses.

'I think,' says Dad Bantelmann at last, 'we should all go inside.'

'I don't know,' says Fridz's mother. But then Fridz disentangles herself from her and she's already on her way to the door of number 17a.

'Great,' she says. 'Konrad, will you show me your room?'

But her mother pulls her back.

'At least have a cup of coffee, after all the fuss,' says Konrad's mum.

'Well, okay, but only a coffee.'

Ten minutes later they're all sitting in the Bantelmanns' living room stirring their coffee. The houses are so alike. They'd said that already in the hall. And at the same time, they're so differennt. It's the way they're decorated, of course. And then someone remarks that the Bantelmanns' banister has an extra rail for little people. Specially made. Very sensible.

Now it's quiet again. The children have got drinking chocolate, and Konrad wishes with all his heart that Peter would knock his over. The hue and cry that would cause would be better than this silence. But Peter drinks his chocolate more carefully than he has ever done before in his whole life.

Something finally occurs to Konrad.

'Thanks for the mobile,' he says, giving it back to Dad.

Dad says, 'You're welcome' and slips it into his pocket.

More silence.

Then they can suddenly hear people going up and down the stairs in number 17b. They've never heard that before. It was never so quiet before in the Bantelmanns'. They all look in the direction of the noise as if expecting an enraged herd of buffalo to come charging towards them. But this doesn't happen. Unfortunately.

'And the rabbit, Friederike, where is it?' It's the man

Konrad doesn't know, though he has a shrewd idea who he might be. 'Did it run away from you?'

'Not from us,' says Fridz. 'We're rabbit transportation professionals. We sold Paul.'

She gets the voucher out of her rucksack, the one she got from the cook. 'We swapped him for a pancake voucher.'

'Hmm,' says the man. 'I see.' He laughs, but it doesn't sound a bit nice.

Fridz's mother also wants to laugh, but she puts a hand up to her mouth and then she looks serious again.

'And what else?' she says. 'What else have you been doing?'

'We were in four different department stores,' says Fridz. She pokes around in her rucksack. 'In one of them, I bought a new pencil case, in the next one, a really sweet key ring, and in the third, a hair slide with a butterfly on it.' She puts them all together on the Bantelmanns' coffee table. 'In the fourth store, Konrad almost bought himself an eraser. But only nearly. D'you know, Konrad is actually very picky, when it comes to erasers.'

Now it's the Bantelmann parents who have to laugh, but they both pretend they just need to cough a little. Then they look very serious again too.

And then there's more silence. It lasts such a long time, that no one even dares to stir their coffee.

'Well,' says Fridz's mother. 'I think we ought to be going. There's lots to be done at home.'

'True,' says Fridz. 'For example, we could get rid of the hutch out of the garage, so our car can sleep in there.'

'Well, then,' says the man, standing up and murmuring something that Konrad can't understand. Then the three of them head for the door, Fridz, her mother and the man who is her father. The Bantelmanns go with them.

'Bye,' says Fridz.

'Bye,' says Konrad.

'Will you come over tomorrow?'

It doesn't sound like a proper question. It could well be a rhetorical question. But although you don't have to answer rhetorical questions, Konrad says, 'Sure. Of course I'll be over tomorrow!'

And then he watches as the three of them set off towards number 28b, Fridz three paces ahead, then her mum, and behind her, the man who is Fridz's father. Fridz waves, without turning around.

'Dad,' asks Konrad, 'are you two going to get divorced?'

Dad closes the door. 'For heaven's sake,' he says. 'Of course not!'

'But if you did?'

They go back into the living room and sit right down where they had just been sitting.

Peter lookes into his ice-cold chocolate, on which a thin skin has formed.

'Ugh!' he says.

'Don't worry about it,' says Mum. 'But you must tell us what you were doing in town, Konrad.'

Konrad says nothing.

'Hmm,' says Dad. 'We don't want to force you, but we are your parents, and I think we really ought to hear what you were up to today. Maybe you need some kind of help, and we don't know how to help you.'

'I don't need help,' says Konrad. 'Really, I don't.' He's trying to look like someone who doesn't need help.

'Friederike maybe?'

Konrad nods. Then he shakes his head.

'No,' he says. 'She'll be okay. She'll manage.'

'So you're really good pals, then, are you?'

'Oh, well,' says Konrad. 'She is a girl.'

'I see,' says Mum. 'And girls can't be pals?'

Konrad shakes his head again. 'No,' he says quickly. 'I mean, yes. Girls can be pals.' As if any sane person could doubt it!

'That's good, so,' says Mum.

Then there's more silence. Bad, never-to-be-broken silence. Nobody stands up and says: 'Well, then, let's go on as if nothing has happened.' Which wouldn't be quite right either.

Silence.

'Well,' says Dad at last, 'if you don't want to tell us, I won't tell any story tonight either.' He looks as if he's about to go off into a sulk. But he's not really sulking. Konrad knows that.

Peter does not know that. He has a lot to say on the subject of no storytelling, but he has trouble getting the words out in the right order. They're all in a jam in his mouth, and none of them wants to let any of the others out first.

'But,' he says, in a state of great excitement, 'but the forest snake.' And then nothing else.

'Exactly,' says Dad. 'Today, the thrilling story of Anabasis the forest snake was due to end. A surprise ending, which no one could have predicted.'

'No!' says Konrad loudly.

'I beg your pardon?'

'It's not coming to an end!'

'But why not?' Dad seems quite taken aback. 'If the two forest snakes and the spaceship-saver get together and if they can just get the knack of it, they can all go back to the planet, to the planet...'

'Klimbambium,' says Peter.

'Correct – back to the planet Klimbambium. All the researchers would be in a state of shock and humanity would be saved.'

Yes. Of course. Konrad has been thinking for ages that the story would finish like that. Or something like that. It was as plain as the nose on your face. And it's a good ending. Maybe a few more funny things could happen, before the spaceship gets going – and then tomorrow is Saturday, and Dad can get started on another one in bed in the morning.

But, thinks Konrad, anything but that.

'That won't do!' he says, shaking his head.

Dad really is taken aback this time. Mum too.

Konrad wiggles forward a bit until he is sitting on the edge of the sofa.

'We have to,' he says. And then he realises that he's not going to be able to speak at all in a moment. Quick, he thinks. Quick! 'We have to start all over again,' he says, and he's already nearly out of breath. 'It was all wrong. Franzkarl Findouter and the forest snake and Luise and Kristine Crisis and everything. We have to –'

That's it. That's as much as he can manage. Konrad can do nothing any more except cry. There's no reason for it, he thinks. He could be thinking for hours about it and wouldn't be able to say why he has to cry. There's no reason for it. None at all!

Mum stands up. She comes and sits beside him and puts her arms around him. Dad and Peter stand up too, but they don't know where to go or what to do.

Konrad is still crying. His throat hurts, and his eyes hurt, and even his ears hurt. His face feels very hot, even if he doesn't touch it, and he knows that if he tried to stand up, he wouldn't be able to; his legs wouldn't be able to hold him.

Konrad cries for five minutes. At a rough guess.

Mum wipes his tears away and Dad gets him a glass of water. Peter looks as if he's going to cry too, but then he runs up to Konrad's room and down he comes with Mattchoo the mouse, so that Konrad can cry into him. That helps a bit.

After five minutes, Konrad tries to stop crying, and it works.

'What time is it?' is the first thing he says.

Everyone says it's half past twelve.

'Could we do something nice?'

Something nice! Dad has to go to see a man about a dog, and Mum just has to wait until the washing machine has finished spinning, so that she can take the clothes out.

Only Peter has no plans that could prevent him from doing something nice. Which he says.

'Please,' says Konrad. 'For my sake.'

Short silence.

Well, then. Just this once. Mum gets changed, Peter packs his mouse, Lackilug, and Dad takes the washing out of the washing machine, while at the same time making a call on his mobile.

Konrad has nothing to do other than put on his yellow anorak with the silver strips and wait outside the door of number 17a. Finally, all four Bantelmanns get into their Passat: Dad sits behind the wheel, Mum on the passenger seat and the two boys behind on their stupid multicoloured booster seats. But not for long, thinks Konrad. One kilo! After two months of eating pancakes, he'll get there, easy. And then he'll take the stupid seat to the dump. That'll be the day!

So, look, there go the Bantelmanns, driving slowly through The Dransfeld. Thirty kilometres per hour, as required, until they get to the main road.

Stop, signal right – all clear on the main road? – yes, it is, foot down and turn.

Where are they going? To the zoo, perhaps? To the movies or to the theme park? Or right into the jungle, in darkest Africa, on a long and dangerous journey of discovery?

I can't say for sure. From here in The Dransfeld, it's hard to know. I can see just one thing. A handful of tiny scraps of paper fly out of the back window of the Passat. As if someone had torn up a little notebook. A notebook in which was written something that's not so important any more. The scraps of paper fly up into the air.

And guess what? It looks quite merry.